Love's
Peculiar
Nature

ISBN-13: 978-1-7334044-6-4
ISBN-10: 1-7334044-6-5

First Printing, October 2020

Cover design by ThomasMax
Front cover photo by Robert Preston Ward.
Back cover photo of Mr. Furry by Brooke Christl

Author's Website: jimfurry.com

Published by:

tm

ThomasMax Publishing
P.O. Box 250054
Atlanta, GA 30325

Love's Peculiar Nature

James Furry

ThomasMax

Your Publisher
For The 21st Century

Acknowledgments

I would like to acknowledge my editing team, Alexandra Christle, C.J.Wold, Dan Brallier, and Ann Furry, who painstakingly put forth a tremendous amount of time and effort in editing the stories to insure that they are professional and well-scripted.

I want to express my thanks to my beta readers, Christopher Furry, Pam Brallier, Dan Brallier, Mark Rebolini, Mary Rebolini and Dana Ridenour, for helping me make the book so much better. Thank you all so much for your edits, suggestions and feedback.

My appreciation is also noted for efforts of my publisher, who was very amenable to my requests to publish this book and to make it available for internet readers.

I would like to recognize CD Mitchell, a mentor who inspired me to venture into the short story arena. His support was invaluable, and helped me establish my platform for this book.

Sincere thanks are also extended to the Southeastern Writer's Association, which has given me a great deal of support and encouragement for the past several years. At their 2018 writer's conference, I am extremely proud to note one of the stories in this book, The Train Wreck, was awarded a First Place Award for short fiction.

I also want to extend a special thanks to Alexandra Christle for her continuing support and her encouragement to foray into the romantic fiction genre. Knowing me, it was quite a leap of faith on her part.

To the instructors and members of the Southeastern Writers Association, all of whom have provided me so much encouragement and assistance in enabling me to produce a much more professional publication than I could have ever accomplished by myself.

Abandoned Love

Wren Widman straightened his tie and grabbed his briefcase. His secretary had placed the morning newspaper at its usual place on the end table by the door of his law office. He snatched it and rushed out into the hallway and into the elevator, counting the twenty floors as it descended. If he didn't hurry, he'd miss the train, and then there'd be hell to pay with his boss, Bob Alwood. The job required he rush to D.C., persuade the clients to agree, sign the contract, and with luck be back in Newark tomorrow night in time for dinner. His mouth watered just thinking of eating a filet mignon at the local favorite Brazilian steakhouse.

While scampering toward Newark Penn Station, he scolded himself for being habitually late. Alwood's image came to mind. What an ass. You'd think the senior partner would appreciate Wren for nailing the account in the first place.

Dashing into the building, the "Purchase Tickets Here," sign was just in front of him. By the time the agent handed him his ticket, he had fewer than five minutes to make the train. Still, the purchase of a mandatory Starbuck's latte became necessary before climbing up the steps to the train platform.

Fortunately, the engineer had been tardy as well and the train was still motionless on the platform. Wren stepped up to the conductor seconds before the man bellowed out, "all aboard."

"You're one lucky son of a bitch today, mister," the guy scowled as Wren stepped into the passenger car.

Wren bladed his body so as not to bump passengers as he began walking down the aisle looking for an empty seat. He passed a row with an older lady sitting on a seat by the window totally involved in knitting some type of baby sweater. A younger woman with a hoody covering most of her face sat at the far end. She appeared to be asleep. Two men in business suits sat together a few rows ahead, both working feverously on their laptops.

A few rows of empty seats were ahead of him. Perfect. He could catch a few winks and by the time he had awakened he'd be in D.C. He could have a nice dinner at the hotel, get some rest, and be in good shape for tomorrow morning's meeting.

He moved toward an empty seat, but a large box was perched by itself on the window seat of the empty row in front of him. Strange. An unguarded box? Had someone gone to the restroom and left it there? Not very smart.

Crap. What if there was a bomb inside? He shook his head. A terrorist would hardly put a bomb in such an obvious place. Maybe he should tell the conductor. But the guy had been crappy to him when he boarded. Besides, it was none of his business who owned the box. It had to belong to somebody, and they'd be back soon.

As he walked up to the seat by the box, questions continued to rattle his brain. Why not sit next to the box? Who knows? Maybe a sweet young thing would come by and claim the thing and he'd make a new friend. Maybe more than a friend.

Throwing his briefcase in the overhead compartment, he plopped himself down in the aisle seat.

The train began to move, hesitating, then picking up speed as it left the station. Wren breathed a sigh of relief. He shouldn't have gotten the coffee but he needed the boost. He'd pulled the Newark *Star Ledger* out of his briefcase. Folding the newspaper over his knee, he popped open the plastic spout on the Starbuck's cup, took a sip, and then sized up the box again.

It was a very large box, and the top cardboard flaps were folded closed with a small opening in the middle of the box. Wren stared at it for a while. He could take a quick peek inside without even opening the top, although he'd hate to get caught if the owner showed up. He wasn't the prying type, but it was too large for someone to have overlooked and forgotten to take when they disembarked.

The conductor stopped by Wren's seat, took the ticket, and then moved on without saying a word. *Why didn't he say something to me? He surely knows the box is not mine.*

Maybe the owner had asked the conductor if it was okay to leave the box. The conductor hadn't questioned him about the box nor seemed concerned.

No matter. Wren opened up the *Star Ledger* and began reading the headlines of the day. There had been a big heroin bust in Hillside; President Trump was still trying to make a trade deal with China, and the usual stories about the Giants and the Jets consumed the sports sections. He was irritated about an article reporting a woman from Westfield who had locked her baby in her van. The extreme heat in the van had killed the baby even though the mother had only been in a store for a "few minutes." He frowned. People continued to be stupid. How could anyone be that dense?

The train slowed as it approached Philadelphia, and then began moving faster as it left the station, making its way closer to Washington, D.C.

Wren put the paper down, finished drinking the coffee, and put his head back on the headrest to take a short nap. Time to relax and not think about the crap that was going on in the world.

He was in a deep sleep when the water and coffee he had consumed awakened him. He needed to make a quick trip to the bathroom. Still half asleep, he glanced to see if someone had come to claim their box. The object of his curiosity was still there and looked untouched. Strange that it had been left alone that long, nor had anyone even approached it since he had boarded the train. What is going on here? Should I tell someone now? What should I do? I feel like a real dummy, sitting here with a box, not knowing a damn thing about what's inside or who is the owner? The curiosity is killing me.

On the way to the bathroom, what was in the box was becoming an obsession. Instead of a bomb, perhaps there is radioactive materials or poison inside. The conductor would be trained how to handle this situation.

On his way back to the seat, Wren decided he would grab his briefcase, flag down a conductor, and report the box to him. Enough of this he thought, not my package. No one had been near the container to this point and the right thing to do was call the conductor. But as he grabbed his briefcase, a muffled bumping sound came from inside the box. The bumping was followed by a noise coming through the hole in the top of the sealed bin. Wren's eyes narrowed. Did the noise actually come from inside the package? The mind often plays tricks on a person and often the imagination plays tricks with the facts. The sound could have come from someone sitting near him. Wren cupped his chin and contemplated what would cause the suppressed tone. Most definitely, the cry was an animal utterance. Maybe someone had abandoned their pet. Or perhaps someone had gotten off the train without their four-legged friend. Interlocking his fingers on top of his head, Wren struggled to wrap his mind about what he had just heard. Adrenalin flowed through him while the urge to attack the box surged.

Wren plopped down on the seat and immediately looked in the top of the crate. All he could see through the hole was cotton cloth. The carton had become an insatiable riddle. Opening the bin may produce some kind of note or explanation, or even the owner's information written on it. By now, although there still could be packages of poison inside, curiosity compelled him to take a look. A good Samaritan would open it, try to find out the owner, and return it. Maybe, the owner had apparently forgotten it when he or she had gotten off the train in Newark the night before.

Wren lifted the flaps up and, in an instant, the sunshine shone through the train window, casting a bright beam of light inside the box. At that moment, he heard a soft cry. Peering past the opened carton, he saw the blinking eyes of a brown-haired, brown-eyed infant staring back at him. *You got to be fuckin' kiddin' me, a baby? Who the hell would leave a baby on a train in a box? How did this happen?*

Wren's mind stalled. A human being was staring at him. Eyes blinking, disbelief was overcome in the second look, and the realization that a little baby was in fact there. How bizarre. Before he had time to think, the child began crying from the sun shining directly in its face. Beside the blanket, there was a bottle with what Wren assumed was milk in it. Completely ignorant of handling toddlers, he did what made sense to him. Holding the bottle just away from the baby's mouth, the baby recognized the nipple and opened its mouth. The hope was for the baby would know what to do. Disaster was averted when the little one clasped the bottle it its hands and started sucking on the rubber nipple. A neatly folded white piece of paper inside the box caught Wren's eye.

"Whoever finds my little girl please, please, help me, please. I am in a difficult position and need you to take care of her for a couple of days. When I am able to take care of her again, you will be able to find me in Newark at Penn Station. I will be wearing a blue-flowered blouse and blue jeans. You will be able to identify me because I will be wearing a necklace that has a gold heart-shaped pendant with the initials, J. W. I trust you to take care of my child because you were the one concerned enough to find her. I know you will love her and take care of her until I can take her back. Her name is Jenny."

Mulling over the situation, Wren's mind was working overtime. What in God's name? What the hell kind of mother gives up her kid to any schmuck who happens to find her on a train. Doesn't she love this child? At least she had enough sense not to dump the kid in a trash container or throw her out of a second story window or leave her in a hot car like the mother from Westfield did. What to do? Will this beautiful being be hauled off to some fat Department of Family Services matron to be ignored in some near empty room. Who knows what would happen then?

He stopped thinking when the train stopped, the engine became quiet, and it stopped moving. Looking around, he saw passengers were rushing off the train. Without thinking, Wren stuffed the note into his sportscoat pocket, lifted Jenny out of her temporary home, shoved her bottle between the papers in the unbuckled opened leather valise, and lifted it off the seat. He pulled out his handkerchief and wiped off the bottle's nipple. Cradling her in his arms, he stepped off the train onto the platform. As he walked through Union Station, much to his surprise, other passengers ignored a man in a business suit carrying a baby with the nipple of a baby bottle sticking out of the top of a briefcase.

The sun felt warm on Wren's face as he walked toward the taxi stand. The smell of baby powder caught his attention. Now full, she appeared content.

"Can I help you with your baby, sir?" the taxi driver asked as Wren approached.

Trying to act like this sort of thing happened every day, Wren smiled at the man. "Oh, ah, my wife had to leave town for a family emergency and I had to come to Washington, so I brought our daughter with me. Thank you, we'll be all right."

Wren was very clumsy buckling the seatbelt around the baby, having never done it before, but the driver seemed to accept Wren's explanation, or on the other hand, maybe cabbies don't give a rat's ass.

"Where to?"

"Crystal Gateway Marriott, please. By the way, do you know if there's grocery store on the way there? I was in such a hurry I forgot diapers and baby food."

The older, gray-haired taxi driver looked at Wren in the rear-view mirror. His suspenders stretched over his striped cotton shirt. With everyone secured, the man's Spanish accent drifted from the front seat as he gave Wren some unsolicited advice, "I have four children and five grandchildren, amigo. Next time you go on a trip, por favor, pack for your daughter and yourself. You need more than a bottle, believe me. There's a Whole Foods Market close to the hotel. I will watch the niña while you get what you need."

The cabbie pulled over to the curb. Wren stumbled as he rushed to get out of the cab. Can I leave her with this guy? He won't leave without getting paid. How am I ever going to get ready for my meeting? OMG, she is crying again. How much longer will she go before I have to feed her again? What the hell am I doing? I don't know how to take care of a kid. What if this guy becomes suspicious and thinks I'm a baby snatcher? I'm just going to grab a bunch of stuff and get back to the cab as soon as possible.

"Thanks mister. I'll be back in no time. Keep the cab running, please. You'll get a big tip. You don't know how much I appreciate it."

"De nada, amigo," the taxi driver smiled, "Don't worry. I will take good care of your little bebe, just like I take care of my granddaughters."

Diapers, baby formula, jars of baby food, an infant blanket, and everything an unexperienced, uninformed, never-a-father could imagine a baby might need was lined up on the checkout counter. Wren put his credit card into the card reader. *Wonder if this all qualifies as a tax deduction or a child care credit?*

As he lifted the armful of bags of baby necessities to leave the store, the cashier asked, "How many babies did you say you had?" Wren ignored the comment and left the store post haste.

Arriving at the hotel, the driver unloaded the bags of groceries while the concierge stared at this man dressed in a thousand-dollar Macy's suit, holding a baby dressed in a pink gown with booties and a pink and black bonnet. There were a half dozen bags of baby items sitting on the pavement outside the Marriott. "I'll have your bags taken to your room right away, sir."

Wren palmed a twenty-dollar bill in the concierge's hand. "You don't know how much I appreciate this, my friend."

A portly middle-aged woman, wearing a Marriott jacket with a badge that said, "Martha" on it, stood behind the hotel counter. Her auburn hair was pulled back in a bun, and as Wren approached and gave his name, she glared at him and the baby. She looked closely at Jenny again. Her blue eyes narrowed and her lips pursed when her eyes focused on Wren. "Your reservation only said room for one. It never mentioned a child. We don't get many businessmen with babies checking in the hotel."

He wiped the sweat from his forehead and around his neck. Things didn't look right. He retold the same story he had told the taxi driver to Martha. This time it sounded smoother and believable, though he was still unsure though whether she bought it.

Wren unlocked the door to room 718. By now, Jenny's arms and legs were flailing and she was screaming at the top of her lungs. He hoped no one would complain, especially to the redhead at the desk. Still perplexed and uncertain, he laid her on the king size bed, raced to the bag of groceries, pulled out a jar, put about half of it on a paper plate, and stuck it in the microwave. Hoping the food would be hot enough, he grabbed a plastic spoon from the cellophane package of eating utensils that was by the coffee pot in the room and scooped a bit of food from the plate onto the spoon. He stuck his tongue out and touched the food to make sure it wasn't too hot. *Hmm, chicken and rice, not too bad.* It was bland, though. Good for a baby.

As the chicken smell filled the air, he carried the paper plate to the bed where Jenny was lying. Her face was scrunched. Wren judged the little girl to be about six months old because she embraced his gourmet meal and seemed to know how to eat baby food. But her satisfaction only lasted for a few minutes before she began to cry again. Wren had done everything he knew to keep an infant content. A large area on the bed underneath her was wet. *Of course, the other half of the equation. She peed herself or worse. Lord, Almighty, what have I gotten myself into? Now I'll be sleeping in a wet bed, too. Guess I'll have to put a blanket on top and sleep on that.* He grabbed a "Huggies" out of one of the grocery bags and sighed.

After several cautious attempts at changing the dirty diaper and finally succeeding, Wren paced around with Jenny in his arms until she fell asleep. The master had succeeded. Wren looked at the baby's closed eyes and partly opened mouth. The quiet movement of her chest told Wren she was in a sound sleep. Her mother must care very little for her. He, on the other hand, as a novice handled well the tasks associated with the sweet angel in his stead.

Exhausted from the stress and the events of the day, Wren pulled out his notes for tomorrow morning's meeting. Despite all the intentions of preparing the presentation, Wren's heavy eyelids closed.

A loud knocking at the door awakened him from his sleep. He knew it. The woman downstairs had called the police. How would he ever explain her to them? He could see himself being interrogated at the downtown police station. Would news of that nature travel to New Jersey? He had made a big mistake bringing her here. Shoulda left her on the train.

He walked to the door. "Who is it?"

"Housekeeping," came a female voice from outside.

Wren opened the door. A smiling young Afro-American woman

dressed in blue scrubs was standing in front of him. "Mr. Widman, the desk had me bring this baby crib up here. Management figured you might need it."

He gasped. "Oh… thank you so much. I do really appreciate it."

The maid wheeled the crib into the room. Her name badge said Tayisha. "You're welcome, Mr. Widman. I'm sure this will make your baby more comfortable. Anything else I can do to help?"

"Nice to meet you. Please call me Wren. And since you asked, I have a meeting tomorrow morning at ten a.m. It should last until about noon. Would you know anyone who might be able to take care of my daughter, Jenny, for a couple of hours? I'd be willing to pay."

She looked at Jenny asleep on the bed. "How much will you pay, Mr. Wren?

"Gees, what's the going rate for babysitters in Washington, D.C.?" Wren had no idea. "She's very special to me, Tayisha. I need someone I can trust. I would pay a hundred dollars."

"For two hours? In that case, Mr. Wren, I don't have to be at work until three tomorrow. For a hundred dollars, I'll be happy to come in early to take care of your little girl."

When she closed the door behind her, Jenny woke up, startled. Wren picked her up, fed her some more baby food, changed her, and then called room service for dinner. While he waited for his food to be delivered, he settled down on the stuffed chair in the room, holding Jenny in his arms. *This is really kind of neat. Imagine what it would be like to be a real father. I could do this.* He touched her hand and she grabbed his index finger and squeezed it. *I think she likes me.*

When the food arrived, Wren put Jenny in the crib, and uncovered the chicken teriyaki plate. Watching Jenny playing in the crib brought a smile to his face. After he finished eating, he picked her up and held her in his arms while they watched the latest NCIS show. To insure she would sleep all night, he fed her one more time, changed her diaper again, gave her a half-full bottle of formula, and put her down in the crib. He muttered, "Now I lay me down to sleep," to her as he silently prayed to himself that everything would turn out all right. Turning off the lamp on the end table, he took a couple of slow, long, deep breaths. The hum of the air conditioner propelled him into a deep sleep.

Morning came in what seemed to be an instant. Wren was in the process of pulling his socks on when someone knocked at the door. Tayisha was right on time. He grabbed his Florsheim's and stuffed his feet into them. The chamber maid was a natural. Must be experienced. In no time Jenny was smiling and laughing. She was in good hands.

The meeting went well. The clients accepted and signed the contracts Wren had brought with him. But at odd moments, he thought of Jenny, the mystery surrounding her, and the horrible mother who'd abandoned her. The fears of being discovered in possession of an unrelated baby were for naught thus far.

He went back to the Marriott, paid Tayisha, checked out of the hotel, and he and Jenny made it back to the train without anyone so much as asking what he was doing with an infant. He was enjoying this unique adventure. Still, his most fond desire was when he arrived back in Newark, this baby's mother would be there when he got off the train. The unexpected chore would be over and he could go back to happy hour at his favorite bar in Down Neck.

The ride home was peaceful. Even the conductor told him what a beautiful daughter he was holding in his arms.

Arriving in Newark, Wren got off the train, the briefcase full of baby things in one hand and Jenny in his other arm. By the entrance of the train station, he stood, holding Jenny. And stood. And waited. Every woman that walked past him wore blue jeans Wren looked closely at every woman to see if she was wearing a necklace with a pendant with J.W. on it. He watched to see if any of them paid particular attention to Jenny. Nothing. After standing about an hour watching and waiting, he caught a taxi back to his apartment, Jenny in tow.

Riding in the taxi, Wren imagined some divorced pathetic woman who had been at wits end and finally abandoned her baby. The sordid wretch was a liar as well by not showing up as promised. He had no choice but to be Jenny's, "daddy" for a while. He looked down and she gave him a big grin and cooed. *She is so cute when she smiles and laughs. Wren tickled her a bit. Makin' a connection.*

* * *

He'd always been a lady's man. Even in law school, many female classmates found their way to him. His smile and smart wit insured he had no lack of female companionship. Early in his career, when he wasn't working, Wren would go to what the guys called meat shops; bars and clubs where singles mingle, hoping to find love, for a while, forever, or just a night. It didn't matter how long to him at the time. It wouldn't be unusual for a young lady to volunteer to go home with him for the night. With him, a myriad of females willing to spend the night was just playtime for a good-looking, smart, young attorney.

Sylvia Winston was a bit different, though. Sylvia was employed at his law firm as a paralegal. Through working several cases together, Wren had developed feelings for Sylvia. Not only his sexual desires, but Sylvia had a personality that he found attractive. They always had a great time when they worked together. There was one big problem though. Wren knew he could not allow the relationship to go far because the firm strictly prohibited employees to date co-workers. The senior partners required all employees sign a condition of employment agreement that they would not have a relationship with any other employee. The firm wanted no part of an affair gone sour resulting in accusations of sexual harassment or a consensual relationship resulting in claims of favoritism among the employees. Nothing was allowed that could result in a lawsuit or bad publicity for the firm.

Wren was determined to make his parents proud that he would be the first in the family to become a successful lawyer, so he would not even allow love to block his budding career. Sylvia had talked frequently about a relationship with him, and he'd been tempted, but he'd made it clear to her that until he became a partner, he wouldn't consider a permanent attachment to any woman.

He and Sylvia would however, have a "working lunch," now and then. They found ways to be with each other, "working together." A couple of times they had met away from work. The attraction had been too strong and so they began a secret relationship. They promised each to secrecy because they both knew that if anyone found out it would mean the end of their jobs at the firm. He would not allow an affair to ruin his career.

***

More than three weeks had gone by and Wren's daily trips to Penn Station at lunch time and after work hadn't produced Jenny's mother. Wren couldn't go on like this forever. He enjoyed having this little girl and was even finding himself taking off time at work so he could take her to a park sometimes and push her in a baby swing, or walk around accepting compliments about, "his daughter." But this temporary situation had to end. I wonder if I could adopt her? I've grown quite fond of her. No, there is too much in my life right now. Don't have time to raise a little girl. I could take her to the Department of Family Services.

How would I ever be able to explain to them how after all this time that I ended up with some unknown woman's baby? I wouldn't want some stranger caring for her. How much trouble could I be in by keeping her for a month? Surely not. What a mess. What to do?

Saturday was another beautiful day. Jenny regularly smiled at him now when he came to pick her up, and now hugged him. He'd grown attached to her. So crazy, he actually had bought a playpen and filled it with stuffed toys. He watched her while she played with a bunny rabbit teething its ear in her mouth. Now and then she would giggle. Drinking a cup of Starbucks latte, he thought about how Jenny had put a crimp into his lifestyle. No clubbing on a Saturday night. No girlfriends lately. And no all-nighters with any woman. Wren couldn't accept the calls or texts from girlfriends because there would be no way he could have any of them over with a baby in the apartment. How could he explain to them this situation? It was an impossible position for him because there was no explanation that could convince any of his friends bringing an infant home he had found on a train was okay. A glass of wine was not appropriate early in the day, but Wren needed to pour himself a glass to help him relax and think things out.

His cell phone began playing a "Man of La Mancha," ringtone. Caller ID posted Sylvia's number. What on earth is she calling me for on a Saturday morning? I hope it's work related. Why is she calling?

"Hello, Sylvia, what's up?"

"Don't know what you are doing right now, but I need you to come over this afternoon."

Sylvia normally sounded happy most of the time when she talked, but this time her voice was deep and pronounced. She seemed nervous and her words were halting.

"What's wrong? I haven't heard from you for a while. It doesn't sound like you."

"I can't explain over the phone. You need to come over right away. There are rumors at work going around that you might have a baby at your apartment."

Wren flinched. When she told him that someone at work was talking about him having a baby in his apartment, he began figuring out what the next move would entail. All of the plans for his career began exploding in front of him. He could feel his face flushing with embarrassment and anger. He had been so careful not to let anyone find out what he had done. If only the mother had shown up as she said in her note. Damn woman.

"I have to take care of something first, Sylvia, and then I'll be right over."

Wren was going crazy. He had to get over to Sylvia's as soon as he could to find out what Sylvia knew. Who told her about Jenny and who else knew? He had to talk to her to try and come up with a plausible explanation that would fly at work.

Wren hit the autodial on the cell phone. He could trust his drinking partner. "Al, I need your help, buddy. I'm not calling to see if you want to go out. I'm asking you for a really big favor. I promise I will pay you back. But you have to promise me you won't tell a soul."

"You sound really strange, Wren. Are you in some kind of trouble?"

He lied. "No, I'm not in trouble. Here's what going on. I'm taking care of a friend's baby and I have to go out for a while. Could you please come over and stay with her until I get back? I promise I'll feed her, change her, and she should be good in the playpen I have in the apartment until I get back."

"What friend would leave her baby with you? Pretty weird, guy. But if you need the help, I'm in. You're goin' to owe me big time. I'll be right over."

"Thanks, Al. I'll make it up to you, I promise."

When Al arrived, Wren rushed into the garage, threw the door open to his BMW Z-4, started it, waited until the electronics cycled, and turned off the car radio. He hit the garage door opener, put the BMW in gear, pulled out of the garage, and lead-footed it to Sylvia in twenty-five minutes for a trip that normally took thirty.

As he fidgeted while waiting for Sylvia to come to the door, all he could focus on was how Sylvia could possibly know about Jenny.

The door opened. Sylvia calmly stood there, her brown eyes wide open, looking directly at Wren. There was a seriousness about her. When he looked back in her eyes, her soul seemed to be reaching out to him. He pulled her close, but she stepped back from him.

"You told me you loved me. Did you mean it or were you just playing me? Take some time before you answer me, and answer me honestly, promise?" Sylvia's stare pierced him like a dagger.

Weird questions she's asking me. Yes, I'd loved her a couple of times but also made it plain to her we couldn't be together as long as we both worked for the law firm. What's this have to do with Jenny? How did she find out I had Jenny?

Wren began, "Yes, but I told…"

Sylvia cut him off. "I know exactly what you explained to me. That's why I submitted my resignation to the law firm this morning."

Sylvia's job had meant so much to her. Wren gaped at her waiting for an explanation. "You did what? Wait? But - but…why?"

Then Wren's gaze dropped from her eyes to her clothes. She was wearing a blue-flowered blouse, Levi's, and a necklace around her neck with a gold pendant with the letters *J.W.* on it.

Suddenly, it all came together, "Sylvia—you—you—are Jenny's mother?" What kind of trick was she pulling? Jenny? Sylvia? The train trip? What the hell was she doing and why involve me? Who else knows at work?

"So, I've been taking care of your daughter all this time, Sylvia? What a horrible trick."

Wren's fists clenched. He was about to lash back at her.

Words began pouring out of Sylvia's mouth. "J.W. stands for Jenny Widman. Actually, you've been taking care of *your* daughter."

Wren just stood there silently as Sylvia continued. "Wren, remember when we would go outside of Newark to secretly meet? And remember those times we made love? Well, after you told me you loved me but couldn't continue the relationship, I tried to distance myself from you. Then I found out I was pregnant.

"I concealed the fact at work by saying I was gaining weight. I started wearing oversized dresses. I made the decision that no matter what happened I was going to have the baby. I told Mr. Pressman I was concerned that all the weight I was gaining could affect my health and asked for some time off to attend a weight clinic.

"I had always gotten top evaluations, so Mr. Pressman was very understanding. I was given as much time as I needed to handle my weight problem. They hired a temporary to handle my work. After Jenny was born, I knew from her birthdate you were the father. I was worried sick you might abandon us. I was afraid I would be left to raise Jenny by myself. I was worried about us."

Sylvia paused to think for a minute and then continued. "I was friends with your secretary and would walk over to her desk and talk sometimes. One day I noticed on the calendar you would soon be taking an overnight to Washington, D.C. I planned on putting Jenny in a box on the train where you might find her to observe how you would react. To be sure she was safe, I sat in the back of the train wearing a hoodie and pretended I was asleep so you wouldn't recognize me. I observed both of you and watched Jenny in case you didn't find her. I followed you around while you were in D.C. watching you and Jenny. I hoped that you would like her and might grow to love her."

"I'm still in love with you, Wren, and I'm hoping that you really love me—and Jenny?"

Tears tumbled down her cheeks. Wren, spellbound and still in shock, flopped down on her living room sofa. He had come to the realization that love for this woman and his daughter was worth more than being a partner in a law firm. He was so ashamed that he had not realized this when he fell in love with her.

"I do love you. I did develop loving feelings for Jenny while taking care of her. Now that I know she's my daughter I want to be with both of you. I'm overwhelmed by it all but I love you both and want us to be together. You had a unique way of introducing me to my daughter."

Wren cradled Sylvia in his arms. "I am so happy you resigned from the firm today. I feel so bad you didn't feel comfortable just telling me when she was born. I am so sorry."

Wren leaned over and kissed her hard on her lips. "Would you marry me? I want you and Jenny to be in my life forever."

"Yes, Wren, forever."

Peculiar Love

The tractor-trailer, with a load of pillows in the trailer, made its way down a snow-packed two-lane road heading south somewhere east of South Bend, Indiana. The driver had strayed off the interstate and was trying to find his way back to his route in the middle of a storm. As the truck's windshield wipers pushed slush from the window, the trucker didn't see the flashing railroad crossing barrier lights until it was too late. He slammed on the brakes but the truck began to skid. It ploughed through the intersection just as the train approached. When the train hit the trailer, pillows exploded into the air like gigantic snowflakes in the storm depositing them all along the rails. Within forty-five minutes, I was having the best orgasm of my life.

***

I never expected to live in a place like Galesburg, Illinois. Growing up in San Diego, California, I loved the perfect weather and the west coast lifestyle. When I married Jeff, I assumed we would have a very happy life right there in San Diego or somewhere nearby. But my husband had searched for jobs on the internet and after a couple of months was contacted by ILPEA Industries, a plastic and rubber tubing manufacturing plant near Galesburg. When he tried to convince me it was too good of an opportunity to turn down, I went along with it, hoping that within a year or two he would get weary and we could head back home.

Well instead, he loved the job. I became less and less happy living in the Midwest. The winters were long and cold, and for at least half of the year snow covered the ground. Although the people there were friendly, I just couldn't bring myself to believe I could stay there long-term. My better half kept telling me I would get used to it, but I had serious doubts. He tried his best to convince me it was a good life by taking me sight-seeing in Chicago, but Chicago seemed even colder than Galesburg. The area suited him well. Good for him. However, I found myself feeling sad and lonely more and more, especially when he went away for a week at a time on business trips.

After a little over three years, our relationship fell apart, at least for me. For some reason, the man who had made me so happy in California appeared to have no clue how unhappy I had become. I had ideas about having a baby, but I wasn't about to start a family in a frozen wasteland. Our relationship had deteriorated to the point where Jeff and I were hardly speaking to each other. I decided I needed to get away for a while just to try and put things back in perspective.

It was late February. Snow and wind gusts were making Galesburg a mess. Of course, Jeff was in sunny Florida meeting clients. My sister, Janelle, who lived in Philadelphia texted me and told me that they were having an early spring there. We've been close all our lives and she is my best friend and confidante. After she told me it was warm in Pennsylvania and I would be welcome to come stay with her for a couple of weeks, I jumped at this opportunity to clear the snow and ease my mind. I immediately began planning my trip.

I refused to drive my car because of the distance and the slippery roads I might encounter. I feared another late-winter storm might get me stuck in an airport, so I dismissed flying there. I was reading the newspaper when I saw the railroad advertised a discount fare and the idea of taking a train ride enticed me. Trains rarely got stuck in the snow and besides the long ride from Galesburg to Philadelphia would give me lots of time to decompress. I called Jeff and told him Janelle had invited me to go visit her. Since I hadn't been particularly loving lately, he readily wished me safe travel.

When I had finished packing my suitcase, I changed into my favorite pair of blue jeans, a flower-patterned blouse, and slipped into my favorite mohair sweater. Grabbing my leather driving gloves, I put on my winter fur-lined hooded jacket, and was out the door to the garage. My Honda Accord struggled to start in the cold, however within minutes I was driving to the Galesburg train station. Thoughts of sun shining through the picture window in my sister's living room filled my brain as the train station got closer and closer. I parked next to a big GMC Yukon that shielded me from the blowing snow. As I walked across the station parking lot, the air was crisp, my nose turned red instantly, and the cold burned my lungs. But I had this sense of freedom, abandoning the town I disliked, and leaving the silent frigidness of my husband for a while to be in the warmth and comfort of my sister's family. I was anxious to see them again, especially their toe-headed four-year-old, Paul, Jr. I was happy for their seemingly perfect family, but jealous, because as much as I wanted to have a baby, I absolutely would not bring a child into this world to live in a place such as Galesburg.

For the discounted price of one-hundred twenty-nine dollars, my reward would be spending the next twenty-nine hours in an Amtrak coach. The trip had me changing trains in Chicago, then passing through stops at Toledo, Ohio and Harrisburg, Pennsylvania before completing my journey. It would provide me with hours to consider my future and whether I would be able to convince Jeff to move back near my mom and dad in California. My hope was that he would find a job there that would make him happy and then maybe we could have a baby.

I chose a coach close to the dining car and asked a passing porter to stow my suitcase. I enjoyed the trip to Chicago and was really happy to be sitting in a heated car. I sat by myself looking out the window at corn fields, barns, and small towns with people walking on fresh snow-covered streets and sidewalks. The rhythmic clickity-clack sound of the wheels of my coach crossing the tracks relaxed me and allowed me to empty my mind of my predicament.

Because of some rough weather along the way, the train was delayed getting into Chicago. I had never been there before and had to find out which train I had to board to make my connection. Retrieving my suitcase, I scanned the big board and found the track where I needed to be. I rushed through the station dragging my heavy suitcase behind me. I was relieved when I saw in the distance the locomotive had not yet departed. I spied a heavy-set porter wearing an Amtrak cap. He smiled as he greeted me. With his big shoulders and well-sculpted arms, he effortlessly picked up my suitcase and followed me as I boarded the train.

"I guess you are used to lifting heavy suitcases," I gasped as I handed him a ten-dollar tip.

"Why thank-you ma'am," he replied. "Always happy to help a pretty lady."

He took my valise and handed me a tag so I could retrieve it upon arrival at my destination.

As I had done on my trip from Galesburg to Chicago, I searched for a car near the dining coach. But this train was a lot more crowded than the previous one. There were hardly any empty seats at all. When I finally spotted one, I quickly grabbed it totally unaware who was around me.

"Have you been traveling very long?" A soft baritone voice spoke.

I turned my head to see a man with a pleasing smile looking at me. My first glance was of a man with a black, neatly trimmed beard and goatee with sparkly green eyes. His wavy black hair contrasted with the red turtleneck and suede jacket he was wearing. I felt my heart beating faster and at that moment my spirit was uplifted. I knew nothing about this stranger but was happy that circumstance had given me this opportunity to sit next to him.

Still caught in the moment, I gave him my best smile in return. "Uh, yes. At least it seems so. But I still have about twenty hours to go. I guess you could say I've just finished the first leg. I never realized there were so many people riding on Amtrak. There was hardly anyone on the train from Galesburg."

Quicker than I expected, his response kept me off guard, "Oh, the news must have traveled fast about this snowstorm. Undoubtedly a lot of people heading east figured the simplest way to go was to take Amtrak. I'm sorry, I should introduce myself since it looks like we will be sitting next to each other for a while. My name is Troy, what's yours?"

"Amanda." I found myself just staring at him. It shouldn't have happened but I found myself attracted to this man. I sat there spellbound.

"Well hello, Amanda." Troy continued, "I'm headed to Harrisburg so I've got a couple of hours less of a ride than you. I normally visit my brother and his family a couple of times a year and could fly, but Amtrak is much more affordable. I always seem to meet some interesting people along the way too. I would expect a lot of people will probably get off at Toledo. However, we will be elbow to elbow until then, if you don't mind?"

Not that I cared. At this moment, I looked forward to it. This kind of stuff only happens in fantasies. I would have no problem spending the next seventeen or eighteen hours with this handsome dude.

"Have you had dinner, yet?" Troy snapped me out of my thoughts.

"Why no, it's about that time. I guess I should head for the dining room."

"Absolutely, it's good to go before the dining car gets crowded. As many people as there are onboard if we get there too late, lots of the food may not be available. I'll get the porter to reserve our seats while we have dinner together."

"Oh, I'm not sure I should do that," I said. "You see I'm married and I'm not sure I should be having dinner with a stranger."

"We're not strangers. You know me and I know you. We're friends. Yes, I noticed your wedding band. Were you aware some women wear wedding rings when they really aren't married just to keep men away?"

"Not me. I have a "for real" husband. I would never think a woman would pull something like that."

I found myself staring at his face again. He looked like a Greek god with piercing eyes and ebony facial hair. I should not accept his invitation but what could happen on a train trip? After due consideration, I accepted his invitation.

"Listen, I promise you I won't put any moves on you. We'll just have dinner. Besides, in the dining room there will probably be people with screaming babies and kids running around dropping dishes and spilling food all over the floor. That's hardly a place for romance."

I would enjoy having dinner with him, no doubt. The prospect of spending time with him was exciting and just plain fun. Fun that I hadn't had for a long time. But I was married and that troubled me.

"Okay, let's do it." *What could one dinner hurt*, I almost said out loud.

I didn't notice any kids running around or babies screaming. It wasn't because there weren't any. I was just focused on Troy. He told me although he had several relationships, he hadn't found the right woman yet with whom he wanted to spend the rest of his life. After downing more glasses of Cabernet Sauvignon that I should have, I found myself telling Troy about all my problems with Jeff, how I disliked boring, cold Galesburg, and how I was desperate to go back home to San Diego.

By the time we finished dinner, there was only about sixteen hours left to travel. Having dinner with Troy was a great way of spending a couple of hours. We made our way back to our coach and the porter, good to his word, had our seats waiting. Troy slipped off his suede jacket and placed it in the overhead bin.

"I guess with so many people on the train, it's starting to get hot in here," he said.

I could think of other things that were making me hot and they had nothing to do with the temperature in the coach. We both had too much wine with dinner and I was feeling so relaxed and comfortable. Suddenly, my mind was in Disneyland, Oz, and the Magic Kingdom all combined. I hadn't felt this good in over a year.

I sat down and within a minute, I felt Troy's hand on mine. I knew I should pull away. I didn't though. Instead, I flipped my hand over and we held hands. It reminded me of the first time I ever held hands with a boy way back in seventh grade. You don't forget things like that. It was so exciting. Nobody in the car noticed or even cared.

"Amanda, I am so attracted to you. I think the attraction is mutual. I know how lonely you are."

It was true. During dinner I told him how despondent and depressed I felt when Jeff was away.

I squeezed his hand and looked into his eyes. I craved his attention, his touch, his words, "Troy, I have never met anyone like you. I know this is plain crazy. I am so attracted to you. You make me feel good in so many ways."

"They say the eyes are the gateway to the heart. I can see your heart. Amanda, I can make you feel so much better if you give me the chance."

Troy turned to me, put his arm over my shoulder, and kissed me. The wine didn't dull the sensation of his kiss. In the middle of the coach with people all around, he kissed me. I felt out of this world. The wine made it all the much better. He kissed me. It had been so long since I had felt anything like that. I couldn't wait and didn't care. I closed the gap between us and we had a long passionate meeting of the lips and mind. My insides swirled and I wanted more.

Suddenly, I heard a lady clearing her throat a couple of seats back. I looked around and now noticed other passengers watching the show. She obviously saw my ring but none on Troy's ring finger, and clearly disapproved. She brought me out of my moment. I could feel myself blushing in embarrassment.

"You are tremendous, Miss Amanda, so wonderful," Troy whispered."

"You too, Troy. I'm really not sure what is going on. I've never reacted this way. It's not me. It seems very peculiar."

Troy had that big brother voice, "My advice, well maybe you just need some time to work things out. You said you were going to visit your sister. Since you trust her and are close to her, you should explain your feelings and bounce things off of her. Then see how she responds. Maybe you and your husband will be able to work things out."

"Thanks. I've had the same thoughts before I met you. I will seriously consider your advice."

Thinking about his suggestion was the furthest thing from my mind. I wasn't even thinking about working things out with Jeff. I wanted to get back up on cloud nine, to escape and go back to Troy's Magic Kingdom. I took Troy's hand and held it tight in the middle of my chest.

Although I didn't mean to, he interpreted my action differently. He grabbed his suede jacket from the overhead and threw it over me, feigning keeping me warm. Then he reached up under my sweater and began unbuttoning my blouse. The touch of his hand on my chest felt so good. I pulled him close and began kissing him again. People weren't noticing as much or perhaps the novelty of it all had dimmed. I found myself wanting to explore Troy.

Again, we were yanked out of the mood when the coach shuttered in an instantaneous moment of slowing down. At the same time, the emergency brakes began screeching and the engineer began frantically blowing the whistle. The sound of the train hitting something ahead blasted in the coach. It lurched forward as the train ground to a stop. Troy and I looked out the window into the night. Just beside the tracks, we saw the most peculiar sight. White pillows were on the ground outside the train, much whiter than the dirty snow under them. Within a minute, people were all looking around in confusion. One passenger said that he heard that the train had hit a tractor trailer at a train crossing. Out of curiosity, people began walking toward the front of the train, trying to see more. As in so many accidents, it seems everyone wants to see the mess. For some reason, people are drawn to things like that. The overhead lights went out from the crash. Within fifteen minutes, Troy and I found ourselves in an empty coach.

We looked at each other realized there was no one around. Spontaneous emotion erupted. There was no time to think. We both unbuckled our jeans and pulled them down to our ankles. Underwear was frantically pulled down. I quickly again glanced around to see if anyone was around. Nobody.

His fingers felt so good inside me and I knew by his breathing that my hands were pleasing him. He pushed me back against the window and I stretched out face up on the seats. His bare ass flung up into the air as he began his rhythmic movement inside me. The excitement and passion ascended. The risk of being caught made it all so much more stimulating. I closed my eyes and experienced the best climax I had ever had. I could tell his orgasm had been as great as mine when he collapsed on top of me, totally relaxed. His breathing began to slow down. With our chests still together, I could feel his heart still pounding but a bit slower. Or was it my heart beating? It didn't matter. I had loved him just now.

There was a peaceful silent moment then we began hearing voices coming our way. The coach lights became activated and all of a sudden, the whole train lit up. Troy jumped off of me, turned over and began pulling up his underwear and blue jeans. Pulling his shirt together, he fumbled with the buttons on his shirt.

I had kicked off my jeans so I pulled them up in a flash not realizing until it was too late that I had forgotten my underwear. With my blouse buttoned, I was in the process of buckling my belt when the porter walked by. Thank goodness he was preoccupied looking at the interior of the coach for damage.

Troy and I did our best impression of trying to make it appear that we had slept through the whole thing. Our looks were hardly convincing when a teen aged young man spotted my pink panties on the floor.

As he picked them up, he loudly announced, "Lose something, lady?"

"Thank you," I tilted my head to the floor, snatched my underwear from him, and stuffed them in my purse.

I watched Troy quickly fall into a deep sleep. That was the last thing I remembered until the next morning. Even though I was in a reclining railroad car seat, I had enjoyed the most satisfying night's rest. The early morning sun and Troy's snoring awakened me. I made my way to the bathroom, relieved myself, and then tried to restore my make-up and hair, not an easy task after the night I had been through. Troy had royally messed up my hair with his hands during our passion, and it took some doing to make my hair presentable. I grabbed an egg sandwich and coffee as I passed through the dining car on my way back to my seat.

My lover was awake when I got back. I kissed him. Why not? He whispered that he loved me and excused himself to go to the bathroom. I sat there thinking about the most incredible experience I had the night before. I felt guilty but I felt love. How peculiar was that? I needed to spend more time with this man to see which way my future would take me or if I had just vented an extraordinary amount of frustration that had built up in my life.

Troy returned with a scrambled egg platter and coffee. After he had finished eating, he told me he never had been to San Diego but if I decided I wanted to move back by myself, he would welcome the chance to visit me. My mind was still foggy from the wine aftereffects. I was so confused, mentally and emotionally. After we talked some more, I knew for sure he wanted to continue the relationship, but I wasn't sure, yet. I explained to him I would take his advice and tell my sister everything. I wanted to be with him.

We were almost to Harrisburg when it occurred to me, I didn't know how to get in touch with him. When the train stopped, he pulled on his coat, grabbed his bag from the overhead compartment, and stood up. I kissed him one last, long, passionate kiss. Then he handed me a piece of paper.

"Here, when you get things straightened out, give me a call if you decide you want to be together. Let me know if you decide to leave Jeff. I love you, Amanda, and if you want me as much as I want you, I would like to be with you like I have never wanted to be with anyone else."

I looked at the piece of paper. *Troy Roman, 312-946-7172, 1425 S. Clarke St., Apartment 202, Chicago, Il, 60605.*

I watched him getting off the train. As I gazed at my handsome guy through the window, he turned and looked back at me. I blew a kiss at him and he mouthed, "Call me, I love you."

The trip from Harrisburg to Philadelphia flew by. My mind was trying to wrap around everything that had happened the day before. It was indeed the perfect love story. I wanted to be with this stranger turned lover and though I was going to have the promised conversation with my sister, I believed life with Troy would be so much better than with Jeff. Jeff could stay in Galesburg for the rest of his life without me and be happy. While waiting for Janelle to arrive, I became obsessed with talking to Troy again. I just couldn't stand it anymore. I wanted–no, had--to call Troy. I searched and searched for the piece of paper he had given me. I was certain I had put it into my purse.

***

The trip had taken extra-long from Chicago to Philadelphia because of the wreck in Indiana. Sam Robinson, the supervising porter was glad he was in Philadelphia, finally. Amtrak was giving him a couple of extra days before he had to work again. Maybe he would take in a Flyer's game. Talking with the cleaning crew, he was able to finally relax while he sipped his coffee. It was strong but refreshing to have in the cold morning. One of the guys from the cleaning crew ambled up to him with something in his hand.

"Hey, Robinson, I found this on the coach floor. Do you think it is important?"

Robinson looked at the writing on the paper. *I wonder who this guy is and why his address and telephone number are on this scrap of paper? Wonder if he was one of the ones taken to the hospital after the wreck?*

Sam Robinson pulled out his cell phone from his belt holster and dialed the number. An answering machine responded, "This is the Roman residence. I am not here to take your call but please leave a message and I will call you back as soon as I am able. Have a good day."

"Mr. Roman, I'm Sam Robinson from Amtrak. One of the cleaning employees found this piece of paper on the floor of one of the cars. I guess it must be yours. If you want it back, you can contact me at 484-412-6934. I hope it wasn't anything important."

Troy Roman listened to the recording, his head exploding. He wondered how many Amanda's lived in Galesburg, Illinois. He hadn't bothered to ask her last name. He collapsed on his couch and wept.

Father's Secret

Lori hitched her brown sorrel, Nellie, to her buggy early in the morning and began her journey west from Petersburg, Virginia to her childhood home at the town of Blacks and White, VA, arriving at her father's house around suppertime. Blacks and White was founded before the Revolutionary War and named after two tavern owners, one by the name of Blacks, and the other by the name of White.

When she arrived, she stalled Nellie in her father's barn. The smell of the dried forage stacked in the corner brought back that familiar soothing feeling she had years ago playing in the hay. A hint of wild onion permeated the air. She grabbed the pitchfork leaning against the wall and threw several forkfuls of hay into Nellie's stall for Nellie to munch on while she visited her father. The long buggy ride had been tiring. She didn't know exactly how many days she was expected to stay there. Papa's letter had arrived a few days before telling Lori he was ill and he needed her to come home. The letter alarmed her because he had written they needed to talk "just in case something should happen." Lori picked out the blue gingham dress that her mother, Annabelle, had made for her before she died. Walking from the barn to the house, she reminisced about the yellow-and-black daisies embroidered in yarn, that adorned the dress. So much time and care her mother had taken to make this dress. Her mother had always told her that if you were going to take the time to make a dress pattern and sew it together, "make it right and make it to last."

It was a bit worn now. Lori was afraid this visit may be the last time Jonas would see the dress his wife had made for her.

The sun produced a spectacular red and gray hue as it began to descend over the back of the house. Lori paused a few moments just to enjoy the beauty of it all before entering the house.

"Daddy, are you up?" she called as she slipped off her wool shawl three steps into the house. Hanging it on the prong on the back of the large wooden door of the coat closet just inside the entrance hallway Lori thought, "No *use wasting time to put this on a hanger. No one will bother it here.*"

A hoarse, hesitant voice called from the kitchen, "Hello, my princess. I'm in the kitchen. Somehow, I've managed to bake biscuits like your mother used to make and I've got vegetable soup on the stove for supper."

Lori entered the kitchen and gazed at her father. Jonas looked gaunt and the thick muscled arms on him Lori had grown up with were now pieces of flab stuck on his bones. When he first looked at her, his eyes lit up and his ever-broadening smile messaged his happiness she had arrived.

"Papa, I hate to see you this way. Are you sure you're eating enough? It's not right for you to live here by yourself this way. I think maybe you should come stay with me, Carrie or Jesse."

Jonas took a ladle out of a drawer and filled two bowls with soup. He put a reed basket covered with a dishtowel on the table.

The old farmer put one bowl of soup down by the chair where Lori was standing and one by the head of the table where he always sat. He removed the dishtowel from the basket to reveal a half-dozen freshly baked biscuits. A French butter dish without a lid was near the biscuits and the butter was soft from sitting on the table for a while.

"Please sit down. Let's eat first before we talk. There are some things you need to know; things I have been holding inside for a long time. Too long."

Lori sat on the plank-bottom chair her father had handmade in his workshop many years ago. She looked at her emaciated, stick-like papa. His sandy-colored hair was scraggly and thinning. His hazel eyes were dull, not focused and alert as they had always been. Whiskers jumped out of his jaw and his furrowed brow revealed years of living a hard life. She remembered how handsome he had looked when her family moved from Pennsylvania after the War. The opaque glass framed picture of her mother and him displayed a young couple happy to be together again after a brutal war.

Her butter knife smoothed the soft butter on the sides of the split bun. It soaked into the little surface crumbs of the cakes. The smell from the steaming soup and the taste of a freshly baked and buttered biscuit brought back memories of family mealtimes from yesteryear, when her father was her hero.

"Eating supper together was always something that was special for our family, that is until your mother died." They ate in silence awkwardly for several minutes.

"I don't think moving in with your family or your sister's family would help me now. I know you would take good care of me, but I don't think I have much time left. Besides, I feel closer to your mother here in this house. I loved her more than anything."

Tears filled Lori's eyes as she hurried to keep busy taking the empty soup bowls, soup spoons, and the bread plates to the sink. She washed them carefully, then gently put them back in the china closet. Her father walked slowly, his face wincing with every step, to the sitting parlor. It pained her to watch him walk that way. She heated a pot of cinnamon tea soon filling the air in the room. Within a few minutes it blended with the distinct smell of burning tobacco. As he always did after supper, Jonas lit a cigarette rolled with his home-grown Virginia tobacco. Even though the smoke had a putrid smell, Lori could close her eyes and see the harvested tobacco hanging in the barn. He coughed several times, his head flinching with each cough.

"Your visits always bring back fond memories," he uttered. "Please come in and sit down. Time is short and you need to know something."

Lori brought the hot tea into the parlor. One of her mother's favorite tin cups was by the end table by where her father was sitting. She guessed he used that one a lot. As she filled the cup with tea, blue smoke filled the room from the burning cigarette. All of the furniture held the smell of cigarette smoke. The room was still much the same as the day she moved out.

She walked over to the window. In the distance she could see a locomotive pulling a coal car, a couple of old brown boxcars with planks missing from the sides, and a caboose down the tracks. She took the heel of her hands and tried to push up the window from the middle sash but the sill was stuck to the bottom of the window. After bumping the sash a few times, she used all of her strength and managed to budge it open a few inches. A cool evening breeze blew fresh air into the room, clearing some of the smoke and making the room more palatable.

"Love to smell the night air," she said to Jonas. "While I was growing up, it always helped me fall asleep so quickly after a long hot day."

Lori watched as her father stared at the picture of her mother and him hanging across from where he was sitting. His gray Confederate uniform, with its gold captain's bars contrasted with Annabelle's pale cotton charcoal dress. It was striking. Next to it, there was a family picture of his mother, brother-in-law, his sister, Annabelle, his three daughters, and him. In those days, photographers asked their customers not to smile and to hold very still because of the slow shutter speeds of the cameras. Even so, after the Civil War, there was nothing to smile about. Yankees had killed her grand-father, her uncle and had taken away all their slaves. Back then, life was difficult for everyone. One former slave, Cody, and his wife, Izzy, came back to work the farm because there was no place for them to go after the war. Cody used to say that now he was free to starve. Eventually, Jonas' brother gave Cody ten acres and Cody and Izzy made a decent living growing tobacco.

Jonas forced a smile, "Sweetie, your mother never wanted me to tell you this, but I decided it wouldn't be fair for me to die without telling the whole story. The first thing I need to explain is that Carrie and Jessie are your sisters, but I am not their father."

Lori's eyes widened in surprise, she stiffened, her fingers began to curl in anticipation of the next words out of her father's mouth.

Her brain filled with confused thoughts and wonder. As she became aware of what had happened, she held her forehead in her hands. Her head nodded back and forth. *Why hadn't she heard any of this before now?* She knew she looked different than her two sisters, but mother always told her different features of parents came out in their children in different ways. Her whole life, when she thought about it, it never gave rise that her features strongly favored her father. The news that Carrie and Jessie were her half-sisters left her dumbfounded.

"Papa, I can't believe you and mama would keep this a secret all this time?"

"Sweetie, your mom loved you so much. She felt things that happened during the war were horrible and shouldn't be repeated. She felt it better for all of us not to keep it in our minds. She tried to protect you from knowing about grisly events people have to endure some times.

Now, Papa's grown little girl was more curious than angry. She moved over to the French settee, and sat on it next to her father awaiting his next pronouncement.

Jonas lit another cigarette and inhaled.

"On the first of July, 1863, about a year before you were born, I was leading my company into Pennsylvania. General Lee decided the best way for us to stop the Yankee invasion was to try and conquer Harrisburg and defeat the Union Army once and for all. We were the best fighting army in the world. Of course, you know how it turned out. Instead of having a battle at Harrisburg, our army suffered a major defeat at Gettysburg.

"That was where I met your mother. I know you think that you have always been a Virginian, but you actually were born in Pennsylvania…and so were your sisters."

Jonas paused, had a coughing fit, and then drew and exhaled another lung-full of cigarette smoke.

"I got separated from my company in the Peachfield battle on July 2nd. There was gunfire smoke everywhere and I got lost. Later, I learned that a lot of the men, a lot of my friends, died there, fighting for Virginia.

He paused for a moment and his eyes rolled back to the left as if he was trying to remember that day.

"While I was walking and trying to find my way back to my company, I felt something hit my left leg. I looked down and realized I had been shot. To this day, I don't know where it came from but I was just happy to be alive. I cut some cloth off a uniform of a dead soldier nearby and tied it tight around my leg to stop the bleeding. I limped along heading toward where I thought was the Confederate line, but…I ended up going the wrong way and fell. I was weak from losing blood. I was confused and didn't know where I was laying.

"I was outside a house behind the Yankee lines. Your mother was in the house, her house, and she saw me outside on the ground. Her husband, Carrie and Jessie's father, who was a Union soldier, was down fighting in Vicksburg, Mississippi with General Grant, attacking the city at the very same time I was on the ground outside his house. I didn't know it, but I was an inch from being dead."

For the love of God, Lori suddenly realized that her sisters' father was a Damn Yankee.

Jonas continued, "I thought she would turn me over to the Yankees right away, but when I woke up, she was looking down at me, staring at me with her beautiful brown eyes."

"What am I ever going to do now?" Those were your mother's first words to me.

"I was in a bed and she had dressed my wounds. But I was in bad shape. The next time I became conscious it was three days later, July 5th, and the battle was over. The Confederate Army had been defeated and General Lee was on his way back to Virginia. I remember being upset I hadn't been killed. At the same time, I was afraid that your momma would turn me over to the Yankees and I would die in a Yankee prison. I remember her taking off my uniform, putting it into a burlap sack and burying it in the back yard.

While she was nursing me, a Union officer visited her, telling her they were looking for Confederate soldiers. She told them I was her husband, sent home to recover before going back to his unit, if he recovered, while crying real tears. She took a big risk that in the confusion of the war, communications would be bad enough that they couldn't easily check it out or that they would just believe her.

Thank God, the Yankee didn't ask too many questions. I think that he was just weary from the battle and was relieved they had won and he was still alive. I was delirious at the time and I remember a foggy vision of a blue uniformed soldier looking at me with a scowl on his face. Had he figured it out, she and I both would have been imprisoned or hanged. Then who knows what would have happened to your sisters."

"Your mother had saved my life, not once, but twice."

Lori was fascinated by this story never heard, but now wondering how she came to be. Jonas's cigarette was down to the stub and he put it out on the wet bottom of his tin cup.

"She went out into the battlefield and talked a Yankee doctor to come to the house and dig the bullet out of my leg. I had a fever for a while but was very fortunate. After I got better, your mother and I began to talk and to know each other better. She told me that when the war started, she prayed to God her husband would join the army. He had a drinkin' problem and would be brutal to her when he got drunk especially when she tried to keep him from beating your sisters. And, she told me he drank a lot. Every day and night. So, when he joined the army, she figured she and your sisters would have some peace for a while.

While he was in Mississippi, she told me she prayed to God that a Confederate soldier would shoot and kill him so he would never come home. She cried when she told me, and she felt wicked and sinful for praying for such an awful thing to happen. She had been so lonely and afraid for the whole time she had been married to him.

But after I had been there for a time, she began to think that even though I was a Rebel, maybe God had dropped me outside her door that day to help her. I had become well enough to leave and I felt it was my duty to go back through the lines to fight with my boys. But she asked me to stay a bit longer.

And then one night right before I planned on leaving, she came to me as I was going to bed. She was standing there, with her hair hanging down over her shoulders, wearing a long white cotton nightgown with the tie open in front, looking like an angel, a real angel from Heaven. I had gone through so much in the war. It had been so long since I had been with any woman. Try to understand if you can. I realized I was completely in love with her by then and I felt I had to help her. All she had to look forward to was that brute coming home, beating her, and beating those little girls. And I wouldn't be there. I held her in my arms. That is the night you were conceived although we didn't know it then. I owed her my life and I told her I wanted her to be with me forever."

It was all becoming clearer to Lori. The war, that damned war that scarred and ruined all of their lives, was now ruining all of her memories about her life, and about her images of her mother and father. Now she knew things she never wanted to know. She had been conceived out of wedlock. Her mother, her beautiful mother, had been unfaithful to her husband."

"Lori, you have to understand, it wasn't something that either of us planned but sometimes life works that way. Things you can't control. Events you can't predict."

Her father reached into his pocket and pulled out his handkerchief, dabbing her tears.

Then he tucked it into her trembling hands.

"There's more."

Lori shook her head and cried. She didn't want to hear any more. It was too much at one time. But her father persisted.

"I wanted you to hear this and please let me finish. The people in town were wondering what this strange man, whom no one knew, was doing at her house. She told them I was a wounded Union soldier she was nursing back to health. She kept telling them I would be going back to my unit soon. But the rumors were vicious. Even though they had noticed bruises on her and your sisters' bodies, and knew that her husband had made frequent stops at the Inn to buy casks of whiskey, no respectable lady would have a strange man in her home with no other male relative in the house.

The postman delivered a letter one day. Turned out it was from her husband. I will never forget the sheer look of fear and panic on her face, the way she swayed on her feet, and how she collapsed on the chair. He had survived the battle of Vicksburg, and he would be home in ten days. We were very happy and in love. She begged me for help. As a southern gentleman, it would have been unacceptable for me to leave and let her face him again, especially when the townspeople began telling him about me. We decided when he arrived home, she would tell him she no longer wanted to be married. With the two of us confronting him, she would tell him she was leaving and taking your sisters with us. She wanted me to stand with her because she didn't know how violent he could be and he would try and kill me. Hysterically, she pleaded that if he had the opportunity, he would not only kill me but kill her and your sisters as well.

The night before he was supposed to arrive home, I dug up my uniform and revolver from the back yard. I cleaned and loaded the revolver hoping it would still work. We held each other close through the night, and your mother gave your sisters a nip of whiskey so they would sleep.

His name was Manfred. When he walked in the door right before noon, he demanded answers from your mother as to why a Confederate soldier was in his house. He was a big man, much bigger than I was or that I supposed he would be. He yelled I was his prisoner and was taking me to the Union camp. I angrily yelled Annabelle told me about how he had beat her and his children and that God had sent me to stop him from hurting them anymore. He screamed she was his damn property and he could do with her what he wanted. She belonged to him and I was just a damned Rebel. His rifle and bayonet were clutched tightly in his hand.

I jumped at him and tried to grab his rifle as he began lifting it up. I was able to grab the end of it before he was able to push the bayonet into me. He was much stronger than me, however, and was able to knock me down on my back. I heard him screaming he was going to kill me. I couldn't hold onto the rifle anymore. Just as he raised the bayonet above me, I heard a gun blast like I had so many times during the war. Your mother had picked up my revolver and pulled the trigger. Thank God, the revolver worked. A bullet struck him in the middle of his back. He fell on top of me, his warm blood flowing from his chest onto me. His breathing slowed and then stopped."

Lori knocked over the chair as she stood and ran from the parlor, flinging herself on her childhood bed. She profusely cried until she fell into an exhausted sleep. She dreamt dreadful, bloody dreams. Her father, the wicked step-father, her sisters, all cowering and crying. She tossed and turned pulling the sheets like twisted demons around her. Her mother, like she had never seen before, was standing there with smoke curling from a gun.

Sometime near dawn, she had a vision of her mother coming to her again, dressed in a long cotton white gown. Sitting on the edge of her bed, Annabelle caressed her head and smoothed her long hair. Then she moved to the rocker, and began embroidering with yarn, yellow and black daisies.

"You have to make it right to make it last" she said, and the dream faded.

When Lori woke up, she felt strangely calm. It would be all right. She understood everything now. It was better to know. The courage it must have taken for her mother to save her sisters and her was incredible. Her loving, gentle, brave father had given her a great life. She put on the kettle for a cup of morning tea to share with her father. He was in the parlor smoking and staring at her mother's picture.

"How much do Carrie and Jessie know?"

Jonas coughed, "Honey, I only had to fill in the blanks. Remember, they were older than you. They remembered the beatings. They remembered almost everything. They never wanted you to know.

"So, what did you do then? How did we get to Black and Whites?"

"We wrapped him in a blanket, put his body in the back of the wagon, and buried him a back field. Months later, your mother reported to the Army she had gotten the letter he was on his way home, but never showed up. She requested that Army authorities try and locate him, but of course we knew they never would. It didn't take them long to declare him missing and presumed dead. Nobody asked a lot of questions during the war with so many soldiers that were killed. For the beatings she took, she deserved the paltry payment she got from the army. After that we were finally able to marry. You were born April 3, 1864. You were just over one year old when the war ended.

It became more and more difficult to live in Gettysburg anymore because with all that had happened, you had been born out of wedlock. Your mother asked her minister to ask God for forgiveness, then she sold the farm. When you were very young, we moved back to my family's plantation. Your sisters readily accepted me as their father, and we were able to enjoy life as a family. I wanted you to tell my grandson and granddaughter that their Grandpa and Grandma fell in love in a most unusual way, and sometimes God acts in mysterious ways. I never would have thought I could find my soul mate in the middle of a war."

Lori went to bed that night thankful she had found out the truth.

It was as though God accompanied her on her visit home. The next morning Lori made Jonas his cinnamon tea, fully intending to talk with him a bit after she hitched Nellie up to the wagon. He had cried out from his bedroom for her to bring the tea to him, saying that he wanted to catch a few more winks before he had his tea. With Nellie hitched and waiting Lori went back to the bedroom. The sun shining in the room caused her to squint. She saw the empty tin cup.

Her father appeared asleep. She reached down and touched his arm. It was cold. Jonas had gone to be with his beloved Annabelle again.

Unorthodox

My freshman year at college had been a blur. My life had become fulfilled my sophomore year when I met the girl of my dreams. I now know dreams can be wonderful until you get awake and realize it was a just a dream.

As I shuffled down the sidewalk my mind wandered in a morose fog. After spring I probably wouldn't see Kelli again until the fall semester. I was employed at the campus bookstore trying to earn money to help with my tuition and she had gone home miles away to Hamilton, OH, in order to also earn money for her tuition. Texting and calling would have to get us through the time away, but I'd rather be there with her all summer. Now, all I could do is dream of us together.

I first noticed her the first week of the semester while I was sitting in the student union, trying to assemble a term paper for my American Lit class. She walked past me; I caught her glancing at me. Out of a polite habit, I smiled. She smiled back. I watched her as she made her way out of the student union and thought, *she might be worth talking to sometime. Something there.* She had wavy brunette hair that fell over her shoulders, blue eyes, and a complexion from a cosmetic ad that used words like "flawless." She left a faint trail of perfume which filled the air around her; one that triggered a pang of guilt inside me. I had smelled that perfume before on Cindy. There was no mistake in my mind, Estee Lauder Sensuous.

When I first left home for college, I thought it best Cindy and I not try to continue a long-distance relationship. I had tried to explain that to her logically but I had strong feelings for her and I knew the words had hurt both of us. She didn't take it well. She cursed me and told me I hadn't tried hard enough to stay together. But for me it was time for us to go in new directions. I did not anticipate the feelings I had for her would follow me to college.

Even after the first few months, I didn't feel comfortable striking up conversations with the women on campus, at least not one that would lead to anything. Accounting was a difficult major for me and I wanted no distractions. For me to get where I wanted, I needed to get great grades. There was no time for females in my life.

By my sophomore year, I was beginning to feel comfortable with the way I was handling my courses, so I figured I could begin looking around for some female companionship. I had been getting letters from Cindy all along, telling me how much she missed and loved me, and wishing we were still a couple. I read what she was writing and looked back at my relationship with Cindy. All the emotions, good times and feelings convinced me I had been in love with her. Maybe it was love but the truth was that time and distance had done for me what it hadn't yet done for her. I just didn't feel the same about her anymore. Marriage was in my carefully laid plans, but by now I knew it wouldn't be with Cindy. My return letters to her were predictably absent of regret or promise with reminders that a long-distance relationship never lasts. When she realized I was serious, she stopped writing to me.

I was sitting in my cost accounting course, but my thoughts were not on the numbers on the board. Instead, the numbers in my mind were the number of prospective brides that were on campus. After all, spring was in the air and love was all around. After the professor dismissed the class I began walking back to my dorm. The smell of freshly mowed grass, the white-dotted blue sky…I thought, *what a great place to be single.* I knew there would be a woman here on campus waiting for me to find her. Falling in love would be easy. Falling in love with the right person may not be easy. But I would find her and we would fall in love. In that, I was confident. We would fall in love. We would both graduate, get married, buy a house, have kids, and live happily ever after.

The thing that I had never told Cindy outright was I was on a mission to find the perfect woman to be my girlfriend and then my wife. My search began my sophomore year. I had taken a couple of girls to the campus dances and had made moves on a few others. Either they hadn't impressed me, or I hadn't impressed them. So, when I saw Kelli again sitting alone in the student union, I thought, *what the heck.* I approached the table where she was sitting as I observed her texting someone. Absorbed in her texting, she had no idea I was next to her.

"Hi there," I sprang on her in a demonstrative tone while trying to get her attention.

At first, she didn't realize I was there or I was talking to her. Her fingers kept tapping the front of her cell phone. Finally, she looked up at me and her puzzled look reminded me we hadn't really "met."

"Do I know you?"

Looking down at her, I caught myself staring at the gold cross resting in the V of her chest. She looked up at me looking at her bosom.

Blushing, I stammered, "Ah, no. I just saw you sitting her alone and wondered if you might want some company?"

"Whatever. As far as I know there are no reserved seats here."

I sat down next to her, now tongue-tied after my idiotic move. My mind was racing, looking for some small talk somewhere in my now-addled brain.

"So, how often do you just walk up to a table, sit down beside someone, and say nothing?"

I felt my face getting warm again, "I'm so sorry. I'm kind of at a loss for words. I couldn't help looking at your beautiful eyes." *Oh, jeez. How corny can a line be?* I tried again. "I have some reading to do for my American History class and this seemed like a good place to study." *Not good, but at least it sounds plausible.*

Words were coming to my brain now. Words like clumsy, uncouth, and awkward.

A big grin lit up her face. "Yeah, I noticed you looking at my 'eyes.' Hmmm, so you couldn't have sat at any of the empty tables to study?"

I looked around. The student union was practically empty. Her grin relaxed me though.

"Actually, I wanted to meet you."

"Pretty unorthodox way of doing it. But then, I like unorthodox."

She looked at me, waiting. Words from who knows where came out of my mouth, "I'm glad you like unorthodox. That's pretty much me. I feel like such a numbskull. My name is Jeffrey Derbach. It's Jeffry Derbach, Junior, actually. When I was a kid, the other kids called me JD. My dad called me Junior. But in high school, everyone called me Jeff." *Ugh, was I babbling?* I took a deep breath, trying not to look like I was taking a deep breath.

"Well hello, Jeffrey Derbach, Jr. Glad to meet you. My name is Kelli McClanahan. I'm a freshman theater major. How about you?" *Oh good. Talk about "What's your major?" I could do this small talk thing.*

I looked at her checkered red blouse and blue jeans. Myriad of thoughts raced through my mind. *She is so composed and mature for a freshman. I can tell she is much classier than me. I love her big gold hoop earrings. I like this one. No, I love this one.*

With my mind back together I began, "I'm a sophomore accounting major. Where are you from?"

"From Hamilton, Ohio, near Cincinnati. How about you?"

"I'm from near Akron, a place called Medina. My father works in the mills there. I'm the first in my family to go to college. I plan on being a CPA someday. And I am not currently seeing anybody, steady, that is." *Whoops, maybe that was too soon. Oh God. I was babbling. No, I told myself. This is small talk.*

My mind was break dancing. *Small talk, but I am attracted like crazy to this girl. Suddenly I believed in love at first sight?*

"Well, Jeff, nice meeting you. You'll never get your studying done if we sit here and talk all day. I'd better go. See ya."

With that, she pushed her chair back, stood, and walked toward the door. I wanted to keep on talking, to keep us together for a while, but in a few seconds, she would be out the door.

"I'd really like to get to know you better, sometime?" I called after her.

She stopped, turned, and looked at me, "I've only been on campus a short time and I haven't been able to get to know too many people here yet but I guess it's okay for us to talk, as friends. But I gotta tell you, I got a boyfriend back home. Really devoted to him. So, friends only, okay?" That last comment, loudly bursting through the air from across the room made me cringe. *Had anyone heard that beside me?* I thought.

Speechless again, I muttered, "That would be great. We can talk, as friends of course." Those immediate thoughts took over. *I shoulda known. Crap. Don't know if I just want to be friends. Plan B, figure a way to get her away from this schmuck. Guess I'll see how it goes.*

Life went on. I made every effort to look for her and bump into her again. Mr. Murphy got in my way and she disappeared for days. At odd times, my thoughts lasered toward her. *I really shouldn't be bothering her since she said she was happy in her relationship. Still, there is something driving me. It should be "us" instead of "he and her."* The love bug had bitten hard.

Saturday mornings are mostly quiet on campus, especially after all the Friday night partying and drinking. But the student council had decided this Saturday morning would be a great time to sponsor a 5K race to raise money for a nearby home for victims of domestic violence. As soon as my eyes opened, I got up, took a couple of Advil tablets with a glass of orange juice, and chased it with a cup of strong coffee, which semi-neutralized my hangover. I was not a very athletic guy, but I figured I could give an hour of my Saturday morning to help some poor beat-up woman. So, I had signed up. Not that I was in any shape to do anything this morning.

At 9:45 a.m., I found myself standing there at the starting line dressed in my Buckeye running shorts and t-shirt.

I felt a tap on my shoulder. Turning my head, my eyes widened when I saw Kelli standing next to me wearing red shorts and a white cotton top which loosely draped her midriff. Her hair was braided in a tight ponytail and even with no make-up she was gorgeous. The smell of Her Estee Lauder Sensuous excited me. *Who puts perfume on to run a 5K?*

"Hey there, JD. Haven't seen you around for a while. Pretty unorthodox to see a guy out here running a race to help domestic violence victims?"

"K-Kelli, hi," was my surprised response. Focusing on answering her question, I added, "You need to know me better. I'm like a pig in a poke. You never know what's inside until you look."

"Well, it's 9:55 a.m. If you want, we can race each other, or we can amble our way for three miles and still make some money for some needy women."

"After last night, I'm more of an ambler, this morning," I confessed.

"Okay, then, JD, let's go."

The official called the runners to the starting line. She and I were way in the rear. I looked over at her, gawking, her ponytail hanging by her neck while she leaned forward on her right leg while waiting for the start of the race. My impulse was to wrap my arms around her body, cup her face between my hands, and plant a solid kiss on her lips. Instead, the official called over his bullhorn, "On your mark, get set, go!"

I hadn't trained for a 5K. As a matter of fact, I hadn't trained at all. So, I began a slow jog. She matched my pace.

"So, where have you been the last couple of weekends?" I queried.

"Hmm, I wouldn't have thought you noticed. Actually, I went home to see my boyfriend. You know to keep a relationship going, you have to see each other as much as possible."

A few people moved past us but winning the race was hardly on my mind. "Everything going okay with you two?"

"Other than missing each other, things are fine."

"Speaking of which, what's your boyfriend's name, anyway?"

"It's Herkimer, not that it's any of your concern. That's my business, not yours."

Herkimer, Herkimer. I stifled a smile and looked away. *Of course, laughing would insult her. Not good for me. Can't do that. Wonder what she calls him? Herky, Herk, or just H? Jeff and Kelli go much better than Herkimer and Kelli. He must be a real winner. I'm so glad she couldn't hear my petty, jealous thoughts.*

"Herkimer, I'm sure he must be very nice. How long did you say you've been going with him again?"

"I didn't say but since you asked, I've been going with him since I was a sophomore in high school, just over three years. He has been very supportive of me going to college. I'm taking Theater Arts because after I graduate, I plan to go to New York and act on Broadway. Herkimer thinks I would be a great actress. I'm actually hoping he'll ask me to marry him soon."

Yuck! Doesn't she realize she could do so much better? Like me, for instance. Herky thinks she would be a great actress? Wonder if that is the only reason he wants to be with her? What was I thinking about? No, it's not right. Then *what does 'right' have to do with it when you love someone? I'm going to put on my cape with the big red "S" on it and save her from Herky the Jerky.*

Making the turn at the one-mile mark, my legs began to strain as I labored to put another foot forward. My lungs were feeling it as well. She looked like she was breathing normally and her gait, although just pacing me, seemed much less labored. It is never a good idea to consume large amounts of beer the night before one runs a race.

"Did you train for this?" I asked, trying not to appear to be totally exhausted.

"No, I jog on a regular basis. You look like you might need a breather," she suggested as she watched my increasingly sloppy gait.

"Me, no. I'm fine. I'm just a little rusty." *May as well change the subject from my non-jogging shape. I had to shield my male ego, although every step betrayed my lie.* I dived in, "I know you are involved with a great guy, but you know there are a lot of great guys out there and you really should go out with a few other guys to know for sure he's the one. Wasn't sixteen pretty young to be deciding to devote yourself to someone for the rest of your life?"

"Well, what kind of guy should I be looking for?" she quizzed.

"There are all kinds of guys out there. You love Herkimer now, but say you graduate and get married to him; who's to say someone might come along who sweeps you off your feet? Then you will regret getting married that young and maybe making a mistake."

"You're not answering my question. I can't think of anyone who would be better than Herkimer. I can't even think of anyone I know now who would even be close to him."

"Well, there could be somebody you know."

"Yeah, who?

"An older, more mature guy, like me, for instance."

With one mile to go, and hearing my last comment, she stopped jogging. She looked at me while three runners ran by us. Her eyes locked into mine. I so badly wanted to grab her sweaty body and kiss her full on her gorgeous lips. She didn't say a word.

"So, when you are running a race, do you often just stop in the middle?" I stopped with her in the middle of the track and posed the question.

"Maybe, I'm unorthodox." She looked at me and smiled. At that moment I knew I had gained a foothold, maybe.

Her smile gave me hope. Maybe she isn't as devoted as she alleges. I don't want to say the clouds parted and angels sang. But I thought, *Old Herky doesn't know it but he's got some competition. If I can ever finish this race without falling over dead, that is. I know I can convince her that her future with me would be so much grander than with old Herky, the slug.*

We began walking again progressing back into a slow jog. My shirt was wet down the middle. Sweat was dripping off my nose and down the side of my head into my ears. I looked at Kelli. There was a little sweat on her brow and some spots of sweat dotted her cotton shirt. We grabbed a bottle of water from the table at the finish line. She sipped it, I guzzled. I was beat. It was obvious she wasn't. Sometimes a man can just tell. I knew she had a peculiar kind of interest in me.

"How about we go over to that cherry tree and rest in the shade for a while?" I tried to look not-sweaty and cool.

"You look like you need it more than me."

"Indulge an old man, will you?"

"You're not that old."

She walked over to the tree and plopped down, leaning against the tree trunk. She pulled her knee up at an angle and rested her foot against a tree root. The bottom of her Buckeye shorts slid up a little when she sat down, showing the length of her bare leg. My heart, which was already

beating up tempo from running, started racing. I slapped my dirty
thoughts away and tried to be a gentleman.

"That was a nice race. Nice to help those in need. I'm going to have
to get back into the habit of regular exercising. You handled it well. You
look marvelous."

"Thank you, sir. I actually enjoyed jogging, if you can call it that,
with you.

She giggled, "I think you are a nice guy. You can be funny, too. Not
too normal, unorthodox. I get to have time with Herk on the weekends,
but I guess having a friend while I'm on campus doesn't hurt. We can
talk more often, if you want."

What? Yes! I tried to be smooth and refined.

"Well, lady, how bout' I go back to the dorm, take a shower, and we
get together tonight? Just to talk, of course. We can just hang out. There's
a sports bar in Columbus. We can go there, listen to the band that plays
there Saturday nights, and talk."

***

Harrison's on Third is a pizza and beer sports bar in Columbus, an
ordinary place etched in my memory now as a place where my love for
Kelli grew. We went there often, laughing and keeping up carefully
schemed light conversations. She kept on insisting we weren't going on
dates because she wouldn't cheat on The Herk. Poor Herk. Of course, we
actually were. He didn't know how much I hated him and loved her. I
was making progress because I noticed she was talking about Herk less.

More often than at Harrisons, I was seeing Kelli outside her dorm,
arguing that Herky was yesterday, I was today. She had this stubborn
devotion to this home town guy. It was getting nearer to Thanksgiving
break and as the holiday and the Herk got closer, she became more
reluctant to go out on these "not-dates." I had to convinced her to go with
me to Harrison's one more time before Thanksgiving break. I had a plan.

We both were underage so we sat at a table, drinking glasses of
Pepsi. We talked and talked and talked. I had a good friend at Sigma Pi
fraternity off campus, so I suggested we grab a small pizza and join some
of my friends at the Sigma Pi house.

She was hesitant, but eventually I wore her down and convinced her
to come with me, so we were off to Sigma Pi. I picked up a pepperoni
and cheese pie and we headed up the street to the frat house. The inside

of Sigma Pi was much the same as in the movie, "*National Lampoon's Animal House*." It was operated by a bunch of fun-loving young men. Saturday nights are a spectacle, meeting every stereotype of raucous drunkenness. By the time we got there, most of the guys were either high or sloppy drunk. Some of their girlfriends were lounging around making out with them and some were drinking with their beaus in the living room. Several were standing talking and drinking in a crowd with music blaring all through the house. We picked our way through the beer cans on the floor, all the while people who were in their own world were on the couch with no idea what show was on the TV. I could tell by the way she was looking, Kelli had never had any experiences that compared to this one.

"Kelli, I'm so happy you came with me. It's getting late and it has been a bit of an unusual evening, but I have had a really great night so far with you and I thought maybe we could celebrate Thanksgiving early."

"Why what do you mean by that?"

"Have you and Herk ever had any beer or wine?"

"You're not going to try and get me drunk, are you, Jeffrey?"

Joey, the Sigma Pi brother who had been my roommate when we were freshmen, had purchased a six pack of Seagram's strawberry wine cooler for me. It was now frosty cold in the refrigerator.

"Of course not. I totally enjoyed being with you, and the perfect way to finish it would be to have some pizza and strawberry wine cooler. Believe me, there isn't enough alcohol in wine cooler to get a mouse drunk."

"I'm not sure I can trust you, Jeff."

"Look, one or two wine coolers won't get you drunk, I promise. Even if it would, I wouldn't do anything you wouldn't want to do. Believe me, it's just like drinking strawberry soda."

"Okay, Jeff, but only a couple. I am famished. We can have some slices with the wine, and then you can walk me back to the dorm. I have to get back early to pack. And I have an Intro to Art final too tomorrow before noon. I could use a little more time to study for it."

I retrieved two wine coolers from the fridge. It was chilled to perfection. I popped the caps off and handed one to her. I lifted the bottle in my hand to my mouth and savored the first gulp before sitting it down on the end table.

"Wow," she said as she sipped from the bottle, "This is really good. It just tastes like strawberry pop. I can't even tell it has any alcohol in it."

We both grabbed a slice of pizza, then another as we sipped on the wine cooler. Half-way into her second bottle, to my surprise, she took a hearty gulp and emptied the bottle, "This is really good."

"Whoa, young lady. You asked me not to get you drunk and I am good to my word. When you finish this one, I'm taking you back to the dorm."

At this point, Joey had given me another six pack, which we consumed in short order. We had a final piece of pizza and I gave Joey a hug for having us over. Kelli also gave him a big hug as we left the fraternity. As we walked back toward the dorm, Kelli was chatting constantly and laughing in between jokes she was telling that weren't funny to me but hilarious to her. I knew the wine coolers had affected her and she was high. I had kept my promise to her and she wasn't fall-down drunk. She was, however, in a very happy mood. Her dorm was just in front of us and I walked her up to the back door.

I stood facing her. I hadn't yet held her hand or done anything she would characterize as crossing the "not-date" line.

"Thank you for going with me. I had a wonderful time talking and just being with you. I really am fond of you, as friends, mind you."

Her eyes sparkled, her face was flushed, and her head cocked to the right slightly. Her smile was ear to ear. It was my time.

"Jeffy, I mean, Jeff, I had fun with you this evening, especially at the fraternity, eating pizza, and drinking the wine. Great stuff, that strawberry wine."

Her words were not making a lot of sense and somewhat garbled as she spoke, "I'm glad you are a genmalman cause I wouldn't wanna cheat on Herk. I won't do it. I will not do it. I will not do it."

All of her actions betrayed her words.

Then she smiled. It was one of those goofy, "I don't care anymore," smiles. I could actually see affection in her eyes. She was wearing a pastel pale green button-down blouse and a denim knee-length skirt. Her dark hair hung freely down her shoulders. I had been wishing for this moment since she first passed by me. Her guard, that rigid guard, was down. She was dead tired, but in a really good mood. I reached up and gently touched her cheek with my right hand. She didn't pull back from me at all. I leaned into her and gave her a gentle kiss on her full lips.

Her eyes widened, "Jeffrey, oh no, I told you that I wouldn't cheat on Herk."

She pulled back a step.

"How did it feel?"

I knew that this would be either the beginning or the end. I hoped with all my heart that it would be the beginning.

She never hesitated. It was her this time who stepped in closer to me, tilted her head back, pushed herself up on her toes, and kissed me. Everything they always told you about a first kiss from someone you love is true. The stars above began to sparkle and fireworks began exploding in my mind. The kiss was solid, passionate, and communicated strong, intimate feelings for me. Suddenly, the conflict in her hit. She pulled back.

"Jeff," she said with a slight change in her demeaner, "I feel so awful. I feel confused. I don't know what I am going to do." But in the next breath, she whispered, "That was amazing. You are amazing."

I was sorry it was so close to Thanksgiving. I had to let her go, let her decide, let her think. She very well may be the one, or not.

"I hope you enjoy Thanksgiving. When Herk is with you, don't forget that I'll be waiting for you when you get back. I love you, remember that."

"How could I forget that?" she responded.

I leaned into her again and we kissed once more. I hugged her and caressed her hair. My body was reacting to her body close to mine. I wanted more than a kiss, "This is to make sure you don't forget."

"Oh my God," she said, heartfelt. Then, reality interrupted, "The dorm mom will be after me soon. Do you have any idea how late it's getting?"

I hoped it was late, too late for The Herk. I hated to walk away.

"Take care. I'm looking forward to seeing where this goes after Thanksgiving." I said, trying for a commitment, but not pressuring her.

She turned and opened the back door to the dorm. As she looked back, she grinned, "I definitely have strong feelings for you. I'm already anxious to see you again."

"Me too," I said as she pulled the door closed behind her, "I will have strawberry wine coolers ready for us when you get back."

She laughed, winked, and then was gone.

***

After we got back from break, our conversation was more open and had grown to include things lovers discuss. Silly things, everyday things, the friends she had on campus, and of course, how much better off she would be with me rather than with Herky. We talked about where we both wanted to go in life, the kind of future we could imagine together and how we could get there. I continually tried to convince her how much better life would be with me than Herk. She was not totally convinced. The time between Thanksgiving and Christmas flew by and every day ended with my anticipation of being with Kelli for as much as possible. Kissing and more than that had become a regular happening. I was hoping that she might invite me home to Hamilton for Christmas, but she told me there was something she had to do before I could go home with her.

The second semester began early in January. I tried to figure out what had been so important for her to do at home, but her texts gave me no clue. I kept texting her during Christmas break in a generic way without using any affectionate words. I didn't know if Herkimer might be near her, and I sure didn't want him to know about me. But it was driving me nuts.

When we both were back on campus, I texted her, telling her I would be outside her dorm in five minutes. I walked into the dorm, passed a group of women babbling away, and sat down on a cushioned chair in the lobby. I played with my fingers and nervously scanned the back hallway watching for her to appear. An old Captain and Tennille song, *Love Will Keep Us Together*, kept playing in my brain. I was feeling great, impatient, high with love and hope.

When I saw her sauntering down the hall from her room, dressed in a mohair sweater and jeans, I stood and rushed toward her. She had the biggest grin on her face. My heart leaped. I had a good idea about what she was about to tell me.

We hugged and kissed, not caring about the group of women now staring at us, making comments under their breath, and whispering to each other.

"I am thrilled to see you. Come sit with me on the couch," she gushed.

"I'm so happy to see you too. I've missed you over Christmas. Did Santa bring you lots of presents?"

Her smile disappeared. "Santa was great to me. I've thought a lot about you and me ever since the night we were at the fraternity and I have to tell you the thing I had to do over vacation."

I held my breath, not even able to think about what was to come next. She sounded so serious.

"I thought about it a lot, and I agree with you. I also had a long talk with Herkimer. I told him it would be best for us to see others while I was in college. If it was true love, we would get back together again. Now I'm free to be with you now and explore what we have without cheating on Herkimer. I couldn't do that, not to him, and not to you."

The big smile reappeared. She reached for my hand. When we touched, I could tell our hearts were finally in sync. Her hands were warm and matched the warmth of our hearts. It was like not only touching skin but touching hearts in ways I never before experienced. We sat holding hands, staring at each other. I leaned over and my lips touched hers ever so gently. I had gotten rid of Herky and captured the heart of the woman I wanted to be with for the rest of my life.

"I love you, Ms. McClanahan."

"I love you too, Jeffrey."

"Herkimer will get over it. I'm certain he will find someone. I'm so excited to have you by myself. And *you* got the better of the deal. You got me." She lit up with her big grin I had come to love.

I glanced at the big clock on the dorm wall. Five minutes to class. Shoot. Not wanting to leave without her, I offered, "Got to get to class. Could you walk with me?"

"I would like to, but I have to get ready for class too. I really have to go back to my room."

"Kelli, it's hard for me to believe, but from the first time I saw you I felt I was in love. Never believed in love at first sight, but it happened with you. Very unorthodox."

"Well Mr. Jeffrey Derbach, Jr., you never passed up a chance to convince me. So, I guess your persistence won me over." She gave me a final smile, said she loved me, and then made her way back down the hallway.

I floated to class certain that whatever the professor preached about cost accounting today would have little success in reaching my brain. I was ecstatic and absorbing the thought of finally being with Kelli forever.

* * *

How do you describe a love addiction that anchors your heart to another and grows stronger with time? Being with Kelli was pure ecstasy. I wanted to be with her every minute of the day. We didn't need to be doing anything but be together. It was life's perfection. On my way to achieving my career goals of becoming a CPA, I was also on my way toward a life together with the only person I wanted in my life. Like St. George beheading the dragon, I had slayed Herky and scattered his remains over the universe. He was gone from our lives forever. It was ironic Kelli had broken up with him much in the same way, I had broken up with Cindy. Long distance romances never succeed. Unorthodox.

* * *

It was nearing the end of my sophomore year and Kelli's freshman year. Kelli and I were solid as a rock, glued together at the heart. We had a mutual commitment and we were planning a future together after college. As my finals were completed one-by-one, I counted down the days until the end of the semester. I became depressed knowing I wouldn't be seeing her for the summer but knew seeing her again in the fall would be so great. We promised one another we would text and talk throughout the summer.

Constantly through June, we texted and called each other. During July, Kelli called less often, telling me that she had gotten a summer job at Dunkin' Donuts and her boss didn't want her using her cell phone while she worked. She also was working extra shifts to make more money. When we would talk, she would tell me she couldn't wait to be with me again in the fall. I was also working extra shifts on my summer job so I knew how difficult it was to keep in touch every day.

In August, I noticed she wasn't texting me as often either. That should have been a clue. However, when I did talk to her, she explained that she would be going with her family on vacation on a cruise and she would not be talking to me because it is very expensive to make calls on a ship. As it was a month away from going back to school, I told her I loved her and couldn't wait to see her in September.

It was excruciating not being able to talk or text her but it didn't matter because we would soon be together once more.

Picture a little puppy, tongue hanging out and tail wagging as it greeted its owner at the end of the day. That was me anticipating holding and kissing Kelli and being together at school once again. I could hardly wait to talk to her in person after what seemed to be a forever summer.

She was going to be living in Dayton Hall this year. As soon I got back to my room in the dorm, I unpacked my clothes, gave a quick squirt of cologne on my neck and scampered off to Dayton Hall.

She was wearing a flower print blouse and jeans, but she now had streaked blonde hair and a pixie cut. I was a little disappointed because I loved her long brunette hair. She looked so…different. As she approached, I noticed that her usual smile had changed to just a sliver of white teeth between the lips. Something wasn't right.

"Hi," she said. "No hugs, no kisses. I need to tell you something."

Without another word from her, like a bolt of lightning out of the sky; it was like the head of a sharp spear piercing my chest. Totally caught off guard I saw on Kelli's left-hand ring finger a diamond ring. Not a ring from me. It was a large solitaire with substantial diamonds accenting it.

My mind was numb as she began to speak, "I wanted to tell you this in person and not over the phone or by text. There was this guy, Bill, who came into my coffee shop every day before closing and would buy an expresso and glazed donut. He graduated last year from Ohio State with an engineering degree. He has a great job. You always told me you believed in love at first sight. Well, I fell in love with him the first time I met him. We love each other so much. He has asked me to marry him and I accepted. This is the engagement ring he gave me. I know this sounds unbelievable to you, especially for the short time I have known him, but I have never been so in love in my life. I always will be in your debt because you were the one that finally convinced me to break up with Herkimer and be with you. I love you, but not nearly in the way I love him. It's the right decision for me. I'm really happy. Bill is my soul mate for life. I feel so sorry for you, but I know you are such a great guy and I know you will find someone much better than me who will make you happy." With all in one continuous heart-wrenching, devastating, monologue, it was over.

I couldn't move. Like a stone statue, I stood in silence, stunned. *What a bunch of crap. I spent all last year desperately trying to get this woman to break up with her boyfriend so I could have her. I was finally successful. I believed I had the girl of my dreams forever. I loved her more than anything in the universe. Now she has found someone else she says she loves more than me. What the fuck?*

Herk and I could have some great talks someday. Maybe we could get drunk together and I could apologize for what I did. Now I know how badly Herk must have felt. So cruel. Of course, I felt much worse for myself. Falling into an endless black abyss and then having the person you love more than anything slamming a lid on top of you? Feelings of absolute rejection and despair filled me. Cindy and Kelli are both happy and here I am? What a cruel thing life can be sometimes. What a crazy thing love is? Why does stuff like this happen?

"Unorthodox."

The Train Wreck

Sometimes the mind is so distorted and confused one just can't take it anymore. Some people would call it going off, others, a break-down. Some say insanity. Whatever it's called, I had had enough. I alternated crying and then pleading to God for help. I would just stare, looking at the plain blue wall before me for an hour at a time, trying to feel anything but miserable.

I had all the reasons in the world to feel this way. I loved her, always. I couldn't even count the number of ways I loved her. I was shattered when Sarah called, telling me she couldn't take it anymore. I believed with all my heart she loved me too. I thought we were happy living in our apartment in Jersey City. I had enveloped myself in my work and including the additional time it took to walk to the PATH train to ride to Thirty-third in Manhattan, and the final trek to my job on Fifty-second, it left few precious moments to spend with Sarah. And now I had lost the love of my life, for how long I couldn't tell. People just don't understand when one's life is permanently put on hold.

My work and the commute to the office became armor shielding me from her. Sarah had packed her things and moved back to live with her mother in Peoria, Illinois, almost a year ago, but I was never able to let go. I faded into a mind-numbing, boring routine. The only variation in my life was my visits to the grocery store when I would pick out my food for the week, usually something easy to cook. And even then, as the weeks went by, the kinds of food became routine, chicken egg rolls, sushi, a weekly Friday night visit to McDonalds, and junk food on the weekends. After a while, everything in my life was routine. My bosses were happy with me because I focused only on work. Occasionally I would think of Sarah and wonder why she never called me, ever. Had I been that horrible to her?

On the PATH train, I would try and find a seat and read the *Star Ledger*, trying very hard to ignore everyone around me. Days didn't count. Weeks didn't count. Nothing counted. Until.

The first thing I noticed were her pale-yellow pumps. Yellow, I guess, because it contrasted with the so many drab pairs of black and brown shoes I saw every day before I opened the paper. My eyes followed the shoes up the nicely shaped legs to the skirt, and then to a matching yellow blouse covered by a black suede jacket. When I dropped the paper to get a closer look, the train stopped and the doors opened. She got off on Twenty-third, the stop before mine. I never saw her face, but as she got off the train, I realized she was the first person in months who caught my interest.

The next day, I actually forgot to buy a *Star Ledger* and spent my time on my ride to work searching to again spy the woman who had caught my eye. I thought it fruitless, of course, because I hadn't seen her face and I had no idea when, or if, she would ever wear that yellow outfit once again. Maybe she was just a visitor to New York and would never ride the train again. Perhaps I really wasn't looking for this strange woman as much as I finally had gathered up the courage to rid myself of Sarah. I didn't know but now I was hoping to see this woman again. I tried to recall the time and day I had seen her before. I remembered yesterday, I had missed my 6:00 a.m. train and had to take the 6:13 a.m. train. I remembered there was the guy with the papers on the corner at the Journal Square and a protest against President Trump's latest deal with Kim Jong-Un was taking place. I decided I would take the same train next Tuesday in the hope that I might see her again.

At 6:13 a.m. I jammed through the doors of the third car of a very crowded train. I grabbed the overhead handrail and held on until the doors closed. The guy I was shoulder-to-shoulder next to me smelled of cheap cologne. I only had about twenty minutes to look for her, but chances of seeing her in this crowded car were slim.

My mind pondered why this mysterious lady affected me this way. It was wishful thinking but I imagined her as a smiling goddess who might be someone who could cause me to love again. Now during every Tuesday PATH ride my hopes would soar when I would get onto the 6:13 a.m. train, but after not seeing her by the time I was ready to take the 5:32 p.m. home after work, my spirits were back down in the sewer.

Weeks passed. Another Tuesday. It was raining hard that night as I walked to the PATH station. I caught the stench of a wandering dog as it darted by me. The streets of New York were a moving mosaic of umbrellas bumping into each other as people scurried home from work. People without umbrellas were crowding the store entrances, trying to keep dry under the overhanging awnings. The intent of the faceless crowd was to get to the subway or PATH train where it was dry as quick as possible. I hadn't paid attention to the weather forecast that day and my Rockports were leaking water into my socks. As I shoved a man in a business suit to force myself into the crowded car, my foot slipped out of my left shoe.

As I bent over to use my finger as a shoe horn to pull the back of my shoe on again, I found myself looking at pair of pale-yellow pumps that were kept dry by heeled galoshes. Could it be? Heart racing, I was determined to get a look at her face. Before I had time to straighten up, the train doors opened, and the galoshes stepped out of the train at my stop in Journal Square.

I hurried off the train behind her, fast-pace walked until I was able to get in front of her and while trying not draw attention to myself or scare her, walked over to the ticket kiosk, pretending to buy a ticket. I heard her steps draw closer and turned. Even through the combined gloom of a downpour torrent outside and the darkened inside of the train station, I locked onto her eyes, big and shiny brown. Her ebony hair was wet, draped on either side of her face, a face that seemed to light up the PATH station. I smiled at her. She smiled at me.

At that moment, for once in a long time, I felt alive again. But I was confused and was so uncertain what to say. Totally flustered, I stood there and did…nothing. She walked out of the PATH station and out of my life again. *Not again*, I thought. I tumbled off cloud Nine and bottomed out, coming to the realization I may never see her again. I followed after her looking all around in the pouring rain, but to no avail. Dejected and soaked, I headed home.

My determined new plan was to take the 5:32 home every day until I saw her again. I was obsessively and emotionally attached to this mysterious woman to whom I hadn't even said a word.

Life seemed to move much faster now since I was no longer only searching for yellow shoes. My life had a purpose again and I was on a mission. Within the week, I saw her again, exiting the train ahead of me at Journal Square. This time I had thought ahead and put my plan in action.

I picked up my pace, closed the gap between us, and when I got right behind her, I tapped her on the shoulder, "Excuse me, ma'am, but would you happen to know where the Belmont Garden apartments are located?"

She stopped and turned towards me. Her expression gave me the impression she didn't really want to talk to some stranger.

"I've heard of that complex. I think it is up around Kennedy, near Newark Ave." She didn't instantly look at me, but when she did glance at me, she asked, "Haven't I seen you before?"

I paused, looking for an answer that wouldn't make me look like a stalker. "We may have seen each other on the train sometime. Do you take the PATH sometimes?"

"Every day. I work in the city," she replied, standing an arm's length from me. She was understandably wary of talking to me.

She was carrying a manila folder. It looked like the binder of a tablet was sticking out of the top of the folder.

"I see you have a sketchbook. Are you an artist?"

"Oh, that. Actually, I like French impressionist paintings. Sometimes I go to the New York library after work, look at impressionist art books, and sketch." At least she had enough self confidence that she wasn't afraid to continue the conversation.

I mused. *She likes art and goes to the NY library. Wow, I don't even know her name, but we have so much in common.*

"Cezanne is one of my favorites. I love Impressionism because you use your imagination to create the story." I offered my hand to her. "Sorry, my name is Les."

"Oh, I'm Julie. I'm sorry, I'm late and I really have to go. Nice meeting you, Les."

"I'll catch you on the train again," I yelled as she walked away. I was back on cloud Nine. I was singing to myself, "Julie, Julie, Julie, do you love me, Julie, Julie, Julie, do you care?"

Walking back to my apartment, I started imagining this new relationship; one that would be better and last longer than the one with Sarah.

The next several weeks were no longer circular or boring. Life was fun again. I felt better than I had in nearly a year. I would say hello to Julie whenever I would see her, and sometimes walk with her through the tunnel at the Journal Square PATH stop. Just small talk but I felt strongly that she was beginning to become attracted to me. It would be only a matter of time until I could ask her for a date.

My plan was working well. I wanted to take the next step with her. I began hanging out by the New York library after work, watching for her.

It was a Friday after work. I was really feeling good about my chances with Julie. I went to a bodega and bought a long-stemmed red rose and made my way to the library. The librarian gave me a look when I entered carrying a rose, but because of all the weirdness that happens in the city, the look was more of curiosity than concern.

I watched as Julie entered the library, following at a discreet distance. Julie went to the impressionist section, picked out a book on Renoir, pulled out her table, and began sketching. I walked up to her and put the rose down on the table next to her.

"Julie, I just happened to see you going into the library. I stopped and picked this up for you. I'd like to talk to you about us."

Her eyes widened and her stare shouted fear. "Les, oh no, you have got it all wrong." She blurted out, "If I took this home, my husband would kill me."

Embarrassed and crushed, I tried to make a joke. "Oh. Your husband. Sorry, I didn't know. We can't have him killing a woman as lovely as you," I stammered.

My husband, my husband, kept ringing in my head as I tried to process this new information. I tottered out of the library and began a mindless run toward the train. With love one disaster in life is enough, but another? I heard in the background Julie yelling she wanted me to come back to her but I ignored her. In the middle of my pain and agony, I struggled to cope with why she hadn't told me she was married.

The PATH station was right ahead of me. For the second time in a year, my mind was in a different place than my body. Losing what I thought were two lovers, my life destroyed once again and having to try and recover once more, was impossible.

***

Julie rushed to the PATH. She was frantically doing her best to catch up to Les. As she approached the standing train, she heard the warning bell sounding that the doors were about to close. Thinking *I must see him*, she squeezed into the train the last second and began searching for Les.

The PATH engineer began pulling out of the Thirty-third Street station when he thought he noticed a crowd gathering by the tracks ahead.

By now, Julie's mind was exploding. *No, Les, you have it all wrong. I was so shocked when you gave me a rose, I was unable to finish before you ran away. I do love you. I am planning on divorcing my husband. That's why I wasn't wearing a wedding band. I've got to find you now and tell you.* Scurrying from car to car she yelled out for him and bumped into other passengers while desperately trying to find him. The car she was in lurched to a screeching stop and Julie fell on her knee grabbing the edge of the seat closest to her to steady her. She had not been able to spot Les.

There was a multitude of shrieks and screams emanating from the crowd outside the train. A man had jumped in front of the oncoming train. Eyewitnesses claimed it looked like a suicide.

Also by James Furry

If you have an interest in what life is really like as a FBI Special Agent, James Furry's biography of being employed by the FBI for more than 30 years, *Fidelity, Bravery, & Integrity, My Story*, is available through Amazon, Barnes & Noble and most booksellers online. To get an your own personally signed copy, you may order at www.jimfurry.com.